AFRICAN
FABLES
&
FOLKTALES

Disclaimer

All rights reserved. No part of this publication may be reproduced, distributed, or transmitted in any form or by any means, including photocopying, recording, or other electronic or mechanical methods, without the prior written permission of the publisher, except in the case of brief quotations embodied in critical reviews and certain other non-commercial uses permitted by copyright law.

This edition is built upon oral tradition and/or available transcripts of african fables and folktales. Credits are listed when available before each stories and are considered a continuation of the copyright page.

For permission requests, write to the publisher, addressed to www.newwordspublishing.com

First Edition

Copyright © 2018 New Words Publishing

Xavier Yebakima

AFRICAN FABLES & FOLKTALES

Stories, Parables and Folktales from all around Africa

New Words Publishing Editions

Contents

Preface vii

1 - How the Hare Helped the Civet 11

2 - Adaka, the Old Man 19

3 - The Monkey's Fiddle 25

4 - The Community Mirror 33

5 - The Turtle and the Man 39

6 - The Mother and the Lion 47

7 - The Leopard and the Rabbit 51

8 - The Two Cold Porcupines 59

9 - The Honey Bird and the Three Gourds 63

10 - Ssebwaato the Hero 67

11 - Why the Chicken Hawk Eats Chickens 73

12 - They Quickly Came with Love and Concern 77

13 - The Jackal and the Spring 81

14 - A Man, A Bird and Ogres 89

15 - A Stubborn Person Sails in a Clay Boat 93

16 - Changing the Face of the Mountain 97

17 - The Dance for Water or the Rabbit's Triumph 101

18 - How the Monkeys Saved the Fish 107

19 - I am the Dancing Man 111

20 - The Guinea Fowl Child (Pitipiti) 115
21 - Two Villages 123
22 - The Story of the Wonderful Horns 127
23 - How the Desert Came to Be 131
Afterword 143
Contact me anytime 145

Preface

How do you enjoy the wisdom and humour of folktales? I have always been fascinated by them. They are such a rich and beautiful inheritance of knowledge passed down from generation to generation, in all cultures. Amazingly, they prove how many facets of humanity are the same throughout time and place, and thus folktales are truly universal literature that anyone, of any age, can relate to.

Blessed with the opportunity to travel around the world, I discovered that South American countries, such as Brazil and Argentina, and the Caribbean islands, have their own versions of African myths. And it is not a surprise that these myths have crossed oceans. From the 1500s, African people were deported from their countries to the Americas and Europe as slaves, and the only thing they could carry with them across the seas was their stories. I still remember listening, with delighted surprise, to the retelling of local myths identical to those I had heard in the Congo or in Kenya.

This project started several years ago when I was looking for tales from African folklore to share with my five-year-old nephew. I dug into old books, discovering stories from different areas of Africa. Some I already knew, but others I had not heard before.

In this book, each chapter starts with an introduction that shares some background about the country that the story originates from. The current delineation of African borders does not match the pre-colonial ethnical organisation, thus the stories may have origins spread across more than a single country. Anyway, my work is not that of a historian but is a joyful sharing of traditional narratives so that you can also enjoy their insightful wit and surprising plot twists. Though deceivingly simple, the tales delve into the core of humanity's condition, exploring themes as diverse as love and loyalty, deceit, jealousy, and revenge. For each story, I have also mentioned the people who, in love with African tradition, made this collection possible by capturing in writing the oral transmission of the tale. Interestingly enough, they were often worshippers of God, with a few exceptions.

So I hope you will enjoy these stories. If you know of other tales or have heard them whilst living in Africa, please write to me about them. Or, if you know other versions of the tales in this book, I would love to hear them. It is important to keep these ancient stories alive so that they are not lost to history, for they remain relevant to people everywhere today.

Love to all,

Xavier.

1

How the Hare Helped the Civet

Introduction

How the Hare Helped the Civet is a folktale from an East African country famous for its vast wilderness: Tanzania.

Tanzania is found in the Great Lakes Region which includes *Lake Victoria*, the third-largest lake in the world. The highest mountain in Africa is also found in Tanzania, *Mount Kilimanjaro*.

It is a dormant volcano with three volcanic cones *Kibo*, *Mamwenzi*, and *Shira*.

The folktale uses animal analogies to impart moral lessons about friendship, cleverness, and foolishness. This story comes from the *Matengo* people, part of the Bantu ethnic group. They originate from the Mbinga District, in the Ruvuma Region in Southern Tanzania.

The language of the *Matengo* people is close to the better-known *Swahili* language. Folklore is rich amongst the *Matengo* and folktales are passed on orally from generation to generation.

Catholic missionaries were the first to write about, and publish folktales, of the *Matengo* people. I selected the version captured by Joseph Mbele, a Tanzanian English professor.

The story tells us of a gullible and naïve civet, a charlatan hare, and a lion who tricks and ultimately gets tricked.

The Folktale

Once upon a time, in the heart of the savannah, there lived a proud and powerful Lion, as well as a wiry Civet. The Civet's coarse fur was striped and blotched in black and white. Black bands around its eyes resembled those of a racoon's.

The Lion was regarded as scary and fearless, but the Civet seemed lazy, sleeping in the fields by day and only waking up at sunset. However, the two animals were good friends. One particular day, when they were waking from a long nap, the Civet said,

> "Whilst we have a pretty good life, it seems to me that there is one thing missing. We do not own any cattle! If

you want to be anyone that matters in this life, you should own cattle. They symbolise your wealth and show your status and power. So, we need to rectify this and buy some cattle at once!"

Now, they did indeed live good lives. The Lion was wealthy, receiving tributes from the community because he was held in more respect than any other lion before him. The Civet was also blessed with good fortune and was a celebrity in town because of his fine fur. Civets coats are as unique to each individual as fingerprints are to humans, making each animal spectacular. The Civet's idea to own cattle was fantastic, and his chest swelled with pride, and he felt delighted by his idea.

The friends travelled to the cattle-market. The Lion looked long and hard for something that would complement his style. He was taking great pride in owning things that would bring him admiration and fame. Therefore because of his dominant and kingly taste, he purchased a mighty bull. The Civet, used to a life of luxury and admiration for his beautiful coat, opted for a splendid cow.

Once they returned home with their new animals, they took good care of them and fashioned them a place to live, complete with feeding and water troughs. The bull and cow did not do very much but eat grass and chew the cud but, the longer they shared the field, the more the bull felt that the cow was very beautiful. The bull and cow's relationship with one another blossomed; after a while, the cow became pregnant.

One day, while the Civet was at the market looking for eggs and vegetables, his cow gave birth to a beautiful calf. The Lion saw a fantastic opportunity to craftily double the number of cattle he had, thus improving his social ranking and achieving instant fame for rearing cattle. Because the Civet was not there, the Lion had his chance. He took the calf, suckling and adjusting to the world around it, and placed it next to his bull lying on the grass. It was now up to the bull to look after it. Then, the Lion closed the gate that separated his field from the Civet's.

The poor calf was distressed at not being next to his mother and was hungry for milk. The cow fretted because her new-born baby was not next to her, and the bull was frustrated by the disturbance the calf was causing.

"I am hungry!" the calf cried.

"The Lion closed the gate! There is nothing I can do," the bull responded sternly.

He was helpless, looking at his child, trying to figure out how to get him back to his mother.

The new-born calf's cries were of no consequence to the Lion. Indeed, the Lion was so happy now to own more cattle than the Civet.

"Okay, child, let us search the field for a way to your mother," the bull said to the calf.

So they walked the field but could not find a way into the cow's pasture. Cows can smell scents from up to five miles away, and the mother cow smelt the food the Civet was carrying back from the market. She called out to her baby and to the bull that the Civet was almost back and that everything would be fine.

Before the Civet had even put the bags of feed down on the ground, the Lion ran to him and, with great feigned excitement, told him,

"Look! My animal has a calf!"

Of course an immediate argument arose between the two.

The Civet puffed out his chest and made himself look larger and thus more dangerous to attack.

> He shouted, "That is my cow's calf, and you are claiming your male bull gave birth to him?". The Civet felt insulted.
>
> The Lion beat off his chest. "My bull did give birth to him, and that calf is mine!" he insisted.
>
> "Bulls can not give birth!" shouted the Civet, infuriated.
>
> "Mine did!" asserted the Lion.

As they were quarrelling, a Hare was loping by with his long back feet. He could not help but hear what they were arguing about, because Hares have big ears, and the ridiculous and loud conversation made his ears prick up. He quickly understood that the Lion was claiming his male bull had given birth to a calf. It was preposterous, outlandish, and plain absurd. The Hare continued his journey homewards, shaking his head and long ears, and pitying the Civet. It seemed terribly unjust that the Lion was making such a claim and deceitfully gaining an animal which he had no right to. He saw no conceivable way that a male, a bull, would ever give birth.

When the Hare arrived home, he sat down and thought about how he could help the Civet. After a while, he came up with a plan. He took his gourds and tied one to each end of a staff, and promptly set off, carrying the staff on his shoulder.

On the way, he met the Lion, who was now in a good mood.

"Tell me, Hare, where are you going?"

"Oh, I am just going down to the river nearby to fetch water for my father who is weak and in bed. He just gave birth to a baby," the Hare answered.

Hearing this, the Lion roared with laughter from deep in his belly.

"Come on now, Hare! Stop being foolish!"

He roared with laughter.

"How on earth could your father have a baby?"

"But the same way your bull gave birth to a calf!" the Hare promptly answered.

The Hare had made him acknowledge his foolish lie. Realising that he had been tricked, the Lion became enraged and flew at the clever animal. The Hare quickly dropped his gourds of water and took to his heels. As you know, hares are very fast, and without the staff's weight to slow him down, he was running very fast. With the Lion chasing him, it was a matter of life and death for the Hare, and he ran as he had never run in his entire life, like cheetahs in the annual animal race.

He thought, "With one snap of his mouth, the Lion could bite me in half."

The Lion was gradually catching up. The Hare saw a dark cave entrance in the distance and decided to head towards it. Once he was inside, the Hare had only a few seconds to figure a way out, or his fate would be sealed by the hunger of an angry lion.

"I have an idea," the Hare said to himself.

As he rushed into the cave, the Hare swiftly jumped onto the ledge near the top. He held his paws up against the roof of the cave, screaming fearfully:

"Help! The cave is collapsing!"

Although this was not the case, luckily, a few pebbles trickled down from off the rocks, making the cave look dangerous and helping Hare's lie. The Lion, following the Hare into the cave, heard him and got alarmed. He too jumped and held his paws up the roof with all his strength. Lions, as you know, are very strong creatures.

> "Now," the Hare said with great cunning. "Hold on, or the cave will crush us both to death. I have an idea to make this task easier. I will go and get some tree branches to help hold up the roof of the cave. In the meantime, hold on tight!"

The Lion stretched his muscles and pushed against the roof of the cave with great effort and strength. The Hare left. He never intended on returning with any tree branches, for there was no need; the roof was strong and in no danger of falling.

After a week, the Hare cautiously approached the cave to have a look at the Lion. He still had his paws pressed to the roof, but he had died from exhaustion. Satisfied, the Hare went to the Civet home and found him next to his cow.

> "Civet, I heard that the Lion was treating you unfairly. I decided to trick him to reveal his lies. Unfortunately, he got enraged and ran after me. I defeated him through my cleverness, and he is dead now."

When the Civet heard him, he rejoiced with all his heart, and sincerely thanked and praised the Hare. Full of gratitude, the Civet gave all the cattle he now owned—the bull, the cow, and the calf, to his hero.

2

Adaka, the Old Man

Introduction

The tale of *Adaka, the Old Man* is an African Parable from Malawi. Malawi is one of the smallest country in South-East Africa, landlocked and bordered by Zambia to the northwest, Tanzania to the northeast and Mozambique to the south, southwest and southeast. One-third of the country is taken up with *Lake Malawi* (also known as *Calendar Lake*). With mountains and small islands, Malawi is also known for its National Parks, and his UNESCO Heritage site *Chongoni Rock Art area*.

This parable uses a story in order to impart a moral lesson to society, about elders and ageing, friendship, youth and having a good attitude, treating others as you would like to be treated, fairness, kindness and hatred.

The folktale may have been relayed many times over the years, but one version of this was collected by Father Renato Kizito Sesana in 1999. This Italian missionary, who has done a lot of work with street children in Eastern and Southern Africa, gathered this story from Malawi. This particular parable particularly resonates with his work with youths.

The story tells the tale of an elder imparting advice to youths. The tale shows his wisdom about people's attitudes and the way they treat others. In the process, a young girl learns a valuable lesson.

Parable

There was an African Village that worked together well as a community. If ever there were any disputes or disagreements, the wisdom of the elders was drawn upon and they were resolved with the help of their mediation and advice. The community worked well together in order to deal with things like harvests, or hunting. This allowed them to have the most amazing communal feasts, with a variety of sumptuous food enjoyed and shared by all.

One day, a wise elder from the village was sat out in a chair on his porch. A young travelling man new to the village passed by. The young man had bright eyes and a sunny disposition. The young man was polite and spoke to the elder with some hesitancy and regret in his voice. He was speaking fondly of his home village, and he said wistfully,

> "I am quite homesick, I have left my family and good friends in my home village. It was a wonderfully supportive community, with people who were wise, friendly, helpful, encouraging. They would do anything for you and there was always someone with a kind word or an ear to listen. There was so much to learn from others, every day afforded a new opportunity to develop. The people were a pleasure to be around and encouraged you to be the best person that you could be. If you needed food, people would help you out, and in return, you would help them when you could. The women in the village were incredibly beautiful, gentle, and kind-hearted."

Adaka The Old Man, smiled warmly which gave him laughter lines at the side of his eyes, and he said,

> "Do not worry young man. The people in this village here, are just as good as those that you have left behind."

After hearing this affirmation, the young man thanked Adaka The Old Man and said how reassuring the advice had been. The young travelling man then carried on his way through the village. He had a determined stride, held his head high and his chest was filled with pride. His heart was warmed by the friendly old man's advice. He felt certain that he would be able to make a happy and content life here in this village and meet lots of wonderful people. It would be a fantastic opportunity for him, and he was sure he would learn a lot from the people he would meet. He was certain to have great new experiences. After a few moments, he disappeared into the crowd of the market, he could not wait, he was ready to start his new life.

Adaka The Old Man continued to sit in his chair on the porch, smoking his pipe. After a short while, another young travelling man passed by. He had hunched shoulders, his forehead was wrinkled in a permanent scowl. He was looking around with suspicion, and he slowly turned to Adaka, looking at him up and down before deciding to approach him, cautiously.

> "I would like to settle in this village, but I was wondering if you could tell me first how the people here are?" the young man asked, with doubt in his voice.

Adaka took a long while to refill his pipe with tobacco, before wisely asking,

> "How were the people in the village you have left?"

The young man sneered.

> "They were very bad people. They were envious and jealous. They never recognized my talent. I am so glad that I left them. I hated it there and could not wait to leave. Everyone was unfriendly, selfish, mean, and unhelpful, only prepared to do things if it would bring them some personal gain."

He almost spat the words out so much he was full of hatred. Adaka placed a worried look on his face, and slowly replied,

> "It would be prudent for you not to enter this Village then. Here the people are exactly the same as those you have left behind. You will not find any friends here."

The young man promptly turned his back to Adaka The Old Man without saying another word . He did not bother thanking him for his advice. The young man headed off down the road, avoiding the village, and went in search of somewhere else that was worthier of his talent, to settle down in.

All the time these conversations have been taking place, Mphande, Adaka's young granddaughter, has been nearby grinding maize using a large flat stone pestle and mortar. Whenever a travelling stranger had stopped to chat with her wise old grandfather, Mphande stopped what she was doing in order to listen to the conversation. She was surprised at the conversations that had taken place.

> "Grandfather, you have lied to the travelling boy! Besides, you gave two completely different answers to the same question."

Adaka The Old Man, the girl's grandfather, smiling, explained his wisdom to her.

> "People are to us what we want them to be.
>
> If we treat them with kindness and consideration, then they will become our friends.
>
> If we despise them and treat them with hatred and scorn, then they will despise us in return.
>
> Do unto others as we would have them do to you.
>
> With this in mind, the first young man will have no problems finding friends wherever he goes. He has a good positive attitude, he will be friendly, trusting, encouraging and supportive and will find likeminded people.
>
> On the contrary, the second young man will make enemies everywhere because that is what he believes them to be. He thinks that everyone is against him, negative, will try to put him down, oppress him and stifle his talent. He is suspicious, surly, and distrusting of

others, so that is what he will find in life.

People do not disappoint you, they are exactly what you look for and expect them to be. If you look for the best in others, that is what you will find. Conversely, if you look for the worst.

Life gives you exactly what you look for. It makes no difference at all what responses I gave to the young men, as the answer to their questions is not in my words, but was already in their attitudes and in their hearts."

Mphande nodded. She started to understand the message that her Grandfather was imparting. It made no difference to where people travelled to. Often people think that moving would give them a fresh start, but this is dependent on their attitude. If they have a bad attitude, it will follow them wherever they go. If they have a good attitude that will follow them wherever they go, bringing them great joy, friendships and wonders.

3

The Monkey's Fiddle

Introduction

The story of *The Monkey's Fiddle* is an African Folktale from South Africa. The country, originally inhabited by Bantu-speaking people, is famous for his landmarks such as the *Great Karoo* and the *Kalahari Desert*.

This tale uses animals to impart a moral lesson to society

about greed, jealousy, theft, and dishonesty. The story was transmitted orally over decades. James A. Honey, a famous South-African folktales writer from the 19th century, recorded this version.

The folktale tells the tale of a Monkey who receives a magical gift. The Brer Wolf is jealous of him. The Jackal takes advantage of the situation. The Lion, the Leopard and other animals make poor decisions. The Monkey exacts his revenge on the lying Brer Wolf, on the Jackal and the foolish animal-court.

The Folktale

Monkey was starving and the land where he lived had no food. Exhausted and hungry he made his way to a new country, where he knew there were opportunities for work and food. In the land he had travelled from, everything was scarce, there were no longer any bulbs to grow plants from, there were no more beans, insects and scorpions were a scarcity.

In this new land, he stayed with his Great Uncle Orangutang who kindly enough offered shelter.

Monkey worked diligently and after he had gathered a decent amount of money, he wanted to return to his homeland. His Great Uncle the Orangutang gave the monkey a bow, an arrow, and a fiddle imbued with magical powers. Uncle Orangutang showed Monkey how with the bow and arrow he would be able to hit and kill anything he aims at. Monkey was glad because it meant he would never go hungry again. His uncle taught him also how to play the fiddle so Monkey could make anything and anyone dance. Monkey was thrilled because he would be forever entertained. In confidence, his Great Uncle told him it could come useful in some other ways too.

Yet, when Monkey returned to his homeland, the very first person he met, was Brer Wolf. Brer Wolf acquainted Monkey with the news from the land of while he was away. Wolf was talking and talking but then got interrupted by a roaring and a growling coming from his stomach like there was a lion inside him. Wolf said he was starving hungry. He told monkey his morning was frustrating. All morning, he had been stalking deer, but he had no luck in catching anything to eat. He had wasted lots of time and energy: his tummy was empty and he was feeling very grumpy.

Monkey feeling sorry for Wolf started to tell him about his bow and arrow that he was carrying at that moment, slung across his back. He told Brer Wolf, that if he could point out a deer to him, he could kill it and catch it without any problems at all. Brer Wolf and the Monkey carefully crept through bushes and trees and spotted a tawny deer in the distance. Monkey took aim with his flawless bow and arrow and killed the deer in the blink of an eye.

Brer Wolf and the Monkey sat religiously and started their sumptuous meal. Monkey thought the food was juicy and tasty. Wolf's heart, however, was burning with envy. He was not thankful for having a full tummy. A feeling of seething jealousy towards Monkey overtook his heart. He wanted to have the same ability to catch any prey with ease. All Wolf could think of was the bow and arrow. He felt that the bow and arrow would make him able to catch any prey.

"Monkey please will you give me your bow and arrow?"

"No, Wolf. This bow and arrow is mine. Great Uncle Orangutang gave them to me. You can borrow them but

I cannot give them to you."

"You do not understand. You do not need them as much as I do. You are a Monkey. You can swing from trees to trees. You can pick bananas. I need it more than you to kill and catch deer."

"No, Wolf. This bow and arrow is mine. Please do not bother me anymore. Bows and arrows are not the means of your race. The way your ancestors hunt, the same way you will continue to hunt."

"If you refuse, Monkey. If you do not give them to me, I shall chase you. I shall take the bow and arrow from your back. I am faster, I am stronger and I am more powerful than you are."

At that moment, a Jackal passed by. Wolf and Monkey decided to use him as a mediator. Wolf was whining and told him that Monkey had stolen his bow and arrow. Monkey furious interjected that the bow and arrow were his. Jackal was at a loss on who to believe.

"I do not think that I am the right person to settle this case. I can not settle your case on my own. We should take the case to the Animal Court of Lion, Leopard and the others. Yet, as you chose me as a mediator, I will personally take care of the object of your quarrel. I will safely look after the bow and arrow until your matter has been effectively solved."

Neither Brer Wolf nor the Monkey really wanted the Jackal to take the bow and arrow. However, they agreed to go to the Animal Court. Each in the pair believed that the court would be on their side and rule in their favour.

Monkey and Wolf went back home, waiting to be called in court. During this time, Jackal had custody of the bow and arrow. He was so happy with the bow and arrow that he started to shot everything in sight. He shot birds and animals. He brought down everything walking and flying in a mass slaughter. He kept on killing throughout a long time until the date when the Monkey and Wolf were called in court.

At the Animal Court, no one believed Monkey's testimony. Leopard and Lion did not believe that Monkey had been given the bow and arrow from his Great Uncle. Lion was sniggering. Monkey had no evidence.

Jackal was then called to testify against. He did so against Monkey. Monkey understood that Jackal lied because he wanted to keep the bow and arrow for himself.

The court ruled that the bow and arrow did not belong to Monkey and that he had stolen them. In Animal Court stealing is a very serious offence, and very wrong. Therefore Monkey was declared guilty, sentenced to death by hanging. Shocked, Monkey yet took a few minutes to regain his senses.

> "I am declared guilty. Well, can I before my sentence, get granted a last request? May I have a last wish?"

Leopard, Lion and all the Animal Court agreed.

> "I would love to have one last play on my beautiful fiddle. Even if you do not believe me, my Great Uncle also gave it to me, and it brings me so much joy to play it!"

The Animal Court agreed and Monkey picked up the fiddle. He was known to be a talented musician in the country. When he started playing the first notes of a well-known song, all the animals in the court rose on their feet. They leapt up from their seats and started dancing in an uncontrollable jig. Monkey was playing faster and faster going to the more lively part of the song. The music from the magical fiddle made the entire court whirling in a frenzy.

Monkey played verse after verse for hours on his magical fiddle. He was engaged and passionate. Some dancers were completely exhausted, several having already felt down onto the floor. The dancers' feet were moving on their own and were tapping and moving to the music.

Monkey was not aware of any of this as his concentration to his instrument was complete. He had his eyes closed and his mouth was singing the same notes he was playing on the fiddle. He had his head leant against his fiddle, and as he played away lost in the music, his right foot was tapping the tempo.

Brer Wolf was the first one to plead to Monkey.

> "Please stop playing Monkey! Please, I can not take any more, I barely have enough breath to speak!"

But Monkey, with his eyes closed, was lost in his musical feat. He was completely oblivious to Brer Wolf pleading and was playing verse after verse the fast and boisterous jig.

Lion too became exhausted. He and Lioness, his wife, had jigged and waltzed around for hours. As they danced past Monkey he growled,

> "I will give my whole kingdom to you, but please! Cease to play this fiddle!"

> "I do not want your kingdom, Lion. I am a Monkey and I want to return to my home with my bow and arrow as I am the rightful owner."

Monkey then turned to Brer Wolf, and said,

" I want also Brer Wolf to confess that the bow and arrow is mine."

Brer Wolf had already lost his breath and his feet were bleeding and hurting him. He cried out,

"I confirm I stole it. I stole it! Please stop the music!"

Lion, still dancing uncontrollably, brought to Monkey the bow and arrow, and the mischievous animal stopped playing his instrument.

All the animals in the court stopped dancing immediately when the music stopped. They were all exhausted with their bleeding feet, but they were relieved. They were also terrified by Monkey now. But he had already left to go back to his home with his bow, arrow and fiddle.

4

The Community Mirror

Introduction

The tale of *The Community Mirror* is a true story from Sierra Leone. It is a tropical country of savannas and rainforests on the coast of West Africa, bordered by the Atlantic Ocean in the south-west, Liberia in the south-east and half surrounded by Guinea in the north and the north-east. Two of the most common ethnic groups are the *Temne* and the *Mende*, who speak an English Creole called *Krio*. Some of the country famous landscapes are the *Mount Bintumani*, and the *Moa River*.

The Community Mirror is a story recorded by Anita Kennedy in 1997, whilst it is not a folktale or a parable, it is a true record of events. It shares a valuable lesson about a sense of identity learned from the community and shows a fundamental difference between cultures that place more emphasis on material belongings. It also shows how important traditional communities are in shaping the personalities, morals, behaviour and actions of their people.

It is a story about friendship, personal relationships, community, and how children learn lessons from their elders and peers.

The story tells the tale of a young boy, who was not able to recognize himself in a photograph because he had never seen his face in a mirror. His sense of identity and belonging had been created solely by what he had been told about himself by his family and friends.

True Story

One day a white western lady called Anita was walking back to her home in Sierra Leone. She was back from a nearby village where she had lived working with the community. Over her shoulder, she was carrying a red backpack. The children from her area recognized that red bag immediately, and they knew that she often carried a camera inside. As she was walking down a dusty path, she could hear little children playing high up in a mango tree. They shouted to her as she walked near,

"Anita, Anita, come and take our photos please."

Anita looked up into the tree and saw the faces of several children smiling back down at her from the branches and leaves of the tree, surrounded by juicy ripe mangoes that were just gaining their red-orange colour. Anita thought that the children's faces surrounded by the natural colours of the tree, would make an excellent photo, so she took her camera out of her bag and pointed it up into the tree and took some pictures.

Anita sent the film roll to her brother in Freetown. He got it developed and sent her the photos back, making sure that there was a copy for each child who appeared in the picture. Word quickly spread throughout the village that the photos had arrived.

"The photos are here! The photos are here!"

One of the children, little Mohammed, eagerly led his mother to Anita's home and asked,

"Anita, Anita, do you have the photos?"

Anita replied, "Yes, Mohammed, I have them and I have one for you."

She opened a black plastic box and took out a photo out of a brown envelope. As Mohammed looked at the photo, he was able to point to the other children in the tree, and name each of them, because he recognized them and had seen their faces daily. But he did not name himself.

He stared at one photo puzzled.

"Who is this little boy? I do not remember there being another child from another village, playing in the tree with us?"

His mother pointed to his picture, and gently said,

"Mohammed, this is you!"

Mohammed was shocked, and intrigued, he could not stop looking at himself, because he had never seen himself before. He ran his hands over his head, hair, nose and ears, as he looked at the photo, and smiled as he had in the photo.

Anita was in awe and astounded. She realised that because nobody in the village had mirrors in their homes, little Mohammed could not recognize his own face!

Mohammed had learned his self-identity via how his mother, his friends and neighbours saw him. Based on their comments he learned who he was. All of the people in the village saw themselves through a *Community Mirror*. When members of the community greeted one another and asked,

"How are you today?"

When other people replied,

"I am sorry that you are sick!"

or

"That is not a good thing what you are doing!"

or

"You are very skilled at drawing!"

or

"You can run so fast!"

or

"You are growing tall and strong!"

or

"That is a very kind thing you have just done!"

or

> "You are so helpful!"

They learned about themselves and who they were.

Before Anita went to bed that night, she thought about the events of the day, she thought to herself,

> "If mirrors ever come to the village, I wish they will not make the Community Mirrors disappear."

The Community Mirrors give a true reflection of the personality of villagers. A reflection that is positive, affirming, and corrected when needed to be. They are not based on vanity, shallowness, appearances or stereotypes. They are a beautiful thing.

5

The Turtle and the Man

Introduction

The tale of *The Turtle and the Man* is an African folktale from the Democratic Republic of Congo. Formerly called Belgian Congo, then Zaire, the country is in Central Africa. It is a French-speaking country, heavily influenced by Belgian colonization. The Congo rainforest is the second-largest rainforest in the world. It is a country of plateaus, savannas, mountains, with volcanoes such as

Mount Nyamuragira the most active volcano in Africa. The *Congo River* is the Earth second largest river by volume. Rich in minerals such as gold, diamonds, uranium or coltan the Democratic Republic of the Congo is the home of diverse tribes such as *Mongo*, *Luba*, and *Kongo*.

This folktale uses a story in order to impart a moral lesson to society about greed, fairness, helping each other, but also about cheating and trickery.

The folktale may have been relayed many times over centuries, but this version was collected by Richard Edward Dennett in 1898 in *Notes on the Folklore of the Fjort*. Richard Edward Dennett was an English trader, who worked in the Congo, and whilst there wrote anthropological and sociological books about Central Africa.

The story tells the tale of a greedy Turtle who benefits from the help of other animals but then cheats them out of their fair share.

The Folktale

A Turtle and a Man built a small town, for them to live in. But, because no food had been planted or had grown yet, they were ravenously hungry.

"Let us build a large trap," said the Turtle.

"So that we can catch an antelope."

The Man agreed, and between them, they set to work and made a very large trap indeed.

"This is too large," objected the Turtle.

"Let us divide the trap, and each of us has a trap of his own."

The Man divided it, and the Turtle chose the best trap of the two. The trap was covered with fine leafy branches so that to an unknowing creature it would look like the ground until they stood on it. Overnight the trap was set. The next morning when the Turtle checked the traps, the Man's trap had caught nothing, but within the Turtle's trap was a splendid antelope.

The Turtle, however, was unable to lift the antelope out of the trap. The antelope was too big, too heavy and the Turtle did not have long arms, just short legs with flippers. The Turtle was not about to be daunted by that however, he called all the animals from nearby and suggested a dance.

Whilst they were all dancing, an Ox came from out of the wood, and he wanted to know what all the singing was about. The Turtle explained to him that he had caught an antelope, but because he was unable to carry it to his house, he had called upon the support of his animal friends.

> "Perhaps, good Ox, you would be kind enough to remove the antelope from the trap, and carry it to my house for me?"

"Of course," replied the strong and helpful Ox.

"Please, will you also go and fetch some water?" asked the Turtle.

The Ox trundled down to the river bed and fetched some water, then upon his return cut the antelope into pieces.

> "Next, please clean the plates," commanded the bossy Turtle.

The Ox washed them with delight, happy to help.

> "This is your share of the antelope here, dear Ox, but first you must go into the woods to get some leaves to wrap the antelope in."

While the Ox was away in the wood, collecting leaves. The Turtle piece by piece lifted up all the antelope meat and took it into his house. His house was strong, a bit like a fortress. He then shut himself inside the house.

The Ox returned from gathering leaves and saw that all the antelope meat was gone. He banged on the door of the Turtle's house and asked for his fair share. The Turtle refused to give him a piece and insulted him quite grossly for a Turtle thought Turtles are known to be quite rude animals. The Ox became very angry and told the Turtle that he would destroy his trap so that he would not be able anymore to use it to trap any game and he would go hungry all again.

> "I warn you, not to do that Ox!" warned the Turtle threateningly.

However unbeknownst to the Ox, the crafty and devious Turtle had re-set the trap, and when the Ox put his head in the trap in an attempt to destroy it, he got caught and surely died after a short struggle.

> "Oh, oh, Mr Ox. I did tell you so. I warned you that you should be more careful when you play with Turtle's trap!" said the wicked Turtle gleefully.

Once again, the Turtle called all the animals to a dance, and they sang loudly and boisterously.

This time it was the Leopard who was intrigued by the noise and came out and spoke with the Turtle. The Turtle explained that his flippers were very sore, and therefore he was unable to carry the Ox in the trap, to his house. And that was the reason he had called upon all of his friends help.

> "Would you be kind enough Leopard, to drag the Ox to my house?"

Happy to help the Turtle, the Leopard at once went into the trap, and quickly brought the dead Ox to the Turtle's house.

> "Thank you, dear Leopard. Would you please now go to the river, to fetch some water, and also clean the pots?" said playfully the Turtle.

> "Certainly," replied the Leopard.

The Turtle and the Leopard cooked the entire Ox. The Turtle placed some of the Ox meat to one side and carried the rest into his strong fortress-like house.

> "You should go into the forest and fetch some large leaves, in order to wrap the Ox meat in," suggested the Turtle to the Leopard.

The Leopard went into the forest, and no sooner had he went into the woods than the Turtle came back to take the Leopard's portion of meat, and shut himself into his house.

The Leopard returned and slinked back with leaves for his meat. He looked around and saw it had gone.

> "Turtle, Turtle, where are you? Where is my meat?" he enquired.

> "I have it here dear Leopard," said the Turtle from inside his strong house.

> "Then give it to me!"

"No, the Ox was mine."

"Yes, but without my help, you would not have had the Ox to eat, for you could not reach him. I helped you to get it out of the trap. I fetched water, cleaned the plates, and helped you to cook it."

"Well, regardless, I am not going to give you any," said the Turtle.

"Then I will destroy your trap so that you will not be able to catch any more food."

"Beware you, Leopard! Do not threaten me!"

But the Leopard was more clever and cunning than the Turtle. He was not about to be cheated out of his fair share of the meat by a smaller animal.

"Yes, I will take good care," he said and went off to the trap.

The Leopard went around the trap cautiously without triggering it and destroyed every part of the mechanism. He then placed the rope around his neck, and laid down in the ruins of the trap, as though he had been caught and died.

The Turtle went to look at his trap and was delighted to find the Leopard inanimate with the rope around his neck.

"Ah, I told you so! Why did you not take more care, Mr Leopard?"

He was speaking to the corpse, stretching out his long neck to take a closer look at the Leopard. As he did so, the Leopard sprang up from his prone position and bit the Turtle's head so fast the Turtle did not have time to retract it. The Leopard then got out of the rope and went into the Turtle's house. He looked around for the meat the Turtle had stored there.

The Man who did not witness any part of the story was walking back to his neighboring home and noticed the Leopard going into the Turtle's house. The Man waited for one hour then said to himself.

"The Leopard has been inside for a long time!"

The Man went inside the Turtle's house as he was suspicious and asked the Leopard what he was doing. The Leopard explained how the Turtle had tricked him to pull, clean and cut the game, how Turtle then stole his fair share of the meat, and how he killed the Turtle. The Man agreed with a nod of his head while listening. He concurred that the Leopard was rightful in his actions and that he should consider Turtle's food as his. The Leopard reassured decided to share the remaining of the game with the Man so neither would stay hungry this week.

6

The Mother and the Lion

Introduction

The tale of *The Mother and the Lion* is a true story from Sudan. Sudan is located in North East Africa, with the *River Nile* splitting it in half. Sudan is a country of flat plains and mountains, including the *Marrah Mountains* and the *Dariba Caldera*. *Lake Nubia* also known as *Lake Nasser* in Egypt is one of the largest man-made lakes in the world. The part of Sudan that this story is gathered from is *Torit*, South Sudan, close to Uganda.

Bishop Paride Taban recorded this version of the story, in *Torit*. *Paride Taban* was a Roman Catholic Emeritus Bishop from 1983 to 2004 from South Sudan, and most of his life work was an effort to make peace in South Sudan real.

The story tells the tale of a mother who outwitted a Lion to feed her hungry children. It narrates the hardships of hunger and famine but also recounts a Mother's love for her children, and her determination to provide for them so they do not die from starvation. Out of desperation, she was prepared to face her fears of getting food off a wild Lion. The story also shows the weight of responsibility that a mother has to carry on her shoulders so her children could carry on being children, far from adult worries.

True Story

A Mother in Torit had completely run out of food. She had a family of five children and her husband had died killed during hunting. All the pots in her hut were empty, but only she knew that to be the case. The children simply completely trusted that their Mother would forever provide for them. The family was quite poor but the kids were just unaware of this.

One day the Mother said to them,

> "Children I have to cook, but it will be more difficult for me to do this if you are running around the kitchen under my feet, whilst I am unpacking the dried meat from the pot at the back. So, if you can please go outside to play that would be helpful to me."

The children did as they were bid, and went to play outside. The meat pot, however, was completely empty. The Mother filled the cooking pot with stones and water and put it upon the wood fire.

"Children, please come back in, and help make sure that the fire is burning. Dried meat takes a long time to cook."

The children now given the task of cooking meat like their mother, forgot all about their game outside and all about them being hungry. This clever tactic freed the Mother, and she went into the woods to find any food, be it meat or vegetables. But as many people had tried before her in the area, there was little of anything there to find. The basket that she wore on her head to carry provisions remained empty. The Mother was becoming more desperate.

She had been wandering for hours in the woods when she heard a mighty Lion roaring nearby. The Mother was naturally terrified of lions, as she knew how strong and powerful they were, and that she could not do anything if confronted with them. Yet she drew closer to where the Lion was roaring from, and as she glimpsed around the edge of a tree, she could see him. The mighty beast had hunted and brought down a buffalo and was now voraciously devouring it. The Mother was very afraid, but she thought to herself that this was her only chance to get food to feed her children.

She took off a circlet of grass that was on her head to balance the provision basket and threw it at the Lion to distract him. The trick worked and the Lion intrigued by the circlet of grass left the food to play with it like a lion cub. The Mother knew she had to act swiftly. Whilst the Lion pounced after the grass ring, and tossed it in the air with a jerk of his head, she took threw sand over the buffalo meat for she knew that lions do not eat soiled meat. She then quickly hid back behind the tree and hoped she would be lucky.

She was lucky indeed. The Lion returned from playing with the grass ring and throwing it into the air, smelled at the meat and recoiled in disgust because his food was now soiled with sand. After he retreated to a safe distance, the Mother cut heavy parts of the soiled meat and filled them in her head-basket until it overflowed. She rinsed the meat and cleaned from the sand in the river and went back home, taking to her heels.

When the Mother returned, the children were still keeping the fire going. She sent them back outside to play, and then swiftly replaced the stones with the fresh meat she astutely took from the Lion. Her cooking did not take long and the children and her neighbours had plentiful delicious meat to eat for that month.

Only the Mother knew how close they were from starvation this day.

7

The Leopard and the Rabbit

Introduction

The tale of *The Leopard and the Rabbit* is an African Folktale from Tanzania. This story comes from the *Sukuma* people, part of the *Bantu* group. The *Sukuma* is the largest ethnic group in Tanzania and most of the people live in *Mwanza*, near the shores of *Lake Victoria*. There is a museum in *Bujora* called the *Sukuma Museum*, that promotes and celebrates their traditional history and arts.

The term *Sukuma* means the people living in the North.

The folktale uses animals to impart a moral lesson to society, about working together, trickery, cleverness, and gullibility.

The story has been relayed many times over decades. This version has been recorded by the *Sukuma Research Committee* in Tanzania.

The story tells the tale of a hard-working but gullible Leopard, a naive Baboon, and an opportunistic Rabbit.

The Folktale

There was a Leopard who lived on his own in a tiny house which was deep into the jungle. One day, he gave some thought to where he was living and decided to look for a better area. After a while, he found a nice spot that he liked, which was near other animals.

He started to cut sticks to build a new house and went looking around in the woods. There, he collected a big bundle of sticks to build his new home.

Whilst the Leopard was busy gathering material, there was a Rabbit close by watching him. The Rabbit also cut a bundle of sticks and placed them near Leopard's bundle. But, the Rabbit did not tell anything to the Leopard for rabbits are malicious animals.

The next day, the Leopard noticed that there was another faggot of stick next to his.

> "Ooh, there is already a second faggot of sticks there. I wonder who brought it?" said the Leopard to himself.

He looked around and he could not see anyone. He shrugged his shoulders and put down a bundle of sticks he was carrying on his back making the total to three on the ground.

The Rabbit was hiding in the bush, watching the Leopard. He put together a second faggot of sticks and brought it to the site, making the total to four bundles. The Leopard and the Rabbit went on bringing bundles of sticks alternately each on his turn.

The Leopard looked at the pile of sticks and concluded that he had enough to build his house. He began to dig the foundations and after a while, he grew tired and went to sleep. The Rabbit left his hiding in the bush, dug the foundations for another wall and set the poles. Having done that until he was exhausted, he went to sleep too.

Each day that passed by, the Leopard and the Rabbit were building their part of the house which was the same house. They never agreed with each other because they had never met, and never discussed this joint enterprise. Though after a while, the house was completed. The Leopard had built one side, whilst the Rabbit had built the other side. The Rabbit moved into his side of the house first. The Leopard then moved to his side of the house. Not long after that though problems started. The Rabbit had lit a fire in his side of the house and the Leopard was very surprised to see smoke coming from the other side of his house.

"Who has ignited a fire in my house?"

"This is my house," said the Rabbit. "I am allowed to burn a fire in my own property."

"YOUR property? Why this is preposterous," said the Leopard.

"I chose this spot for the house, and I painstakingly cut down sticks every day, carried them here, dug the foundations and built this home."

"I too gathered sticks, carried them here, dug the foundations and built this house," said the Rabbit.

It suddenly dawned on the Leopard where the other piles of sticks had come from. He realised that the extra sticks he had been seeing every day belonged to the Rabbit. The other walls he had seen erected overnight almost like magic, had actually been built by the Rabbit.

The Leopard was stuck in a really embarrassing company, having built a house with an animal he had never met, with no prior consultation or agreement. He had started building the house first, and it was quite inconsiderate of the Rabbit to start building on exactly the same spot.

The Rabbit lived in his side of the house with his entire family but as he was crafty and cunning he wanted the entire house for him and his family. He therefore quickly came up with an idea. He told his wife, Mrs Rabbit, to pinch and squeeze their children's toes to make them cry aloud. When the baby rabbits started to scream, he asked his wife in a big and angry voice,

"Why are the children crying?"

Mrs Rabbit replied, "They are crying because they want some elephant's liver."

The Rabbit was speaking purposely loudly because he wanted the Leopard to hear him. He put on a deliberately boastful voice,

"Tell the children to stop crying. Finding an elephant's liver is no problem for me. Tomorrow I will kill an elephant so that our children can eat his liver tomorrow night."

When the Leopard heard these words, he became extremely afraid. He thought that the Rabbit was a very dangerous animal.

If the Rabbit could kill an elephant that was much bigger than him he could undoubtedly kill the Leopard too.

A few days later, the Leopard and the Rabbit had another argument. The Rabbit thought of another way to scare the Leopard and push him away from the house. The Rabbit told Mrs Rabbit again to squeeze and pinch the baby rabbits' toes so that they would cry. Mrs Rabbit's children started screaming like there was no tomorrow. The Rabbit asked his wife in a loud irritated voice,

"Why are the children crying?"

"Because they want some leopard's liver," replied Mrs Rabbit.

The Leopard could very clearly hear the conversation. Again, the Rabbit was deliberately being loud so that the Leopard could hear him distinctly,

"Tell the children not to cry," said the Rabbit.

"Finding a leopard's liver is no problem for me. In fact, there is a leopard right here in this house with us. I will easily kill him and tomorrow we can feed the children with his liver. I do not want my children to be upset or be deprived of anything."

The Leopard was terrified and he thought to himself,

"I must run away from here immediately. Otherwise, I may be killed by the Rabbit whilst I am sleeping."

When the Rabbit and his family woke up the next day, the Leopard had left and had emptied his side of the house. The Rabbit finally had the whole house for himself.

In a hurry from the house and still running breathlessly since the night before, the Leopard met on his way the Baboon walking on the side of the road.

> "Why are you out of breath, and in such a big rush, this early in the morning?" the Baboon asked.
>
> "Besides why are you carrying all your possessions with you? Where are you travelling to?"
>
> "I am running away from the Rabbit," answered the Leopard. "Because I have heard him devising to kill me and feed my liver to his family. The worst part is that I had to leave the house that I have built with my bare hands!"
>
> "Oh, I know the Rabbit of old," the Baboon replied. "This one is a usual trick of his. Allow me to take you back to your house. Only, to appear as a stronger front we will tie our tails together. This way we will appear joined and together much bigger and fiercer than him."

The Leopard and the Baboon tied their tails together and returned to the Leopard's house. The Rabbit saw them approaching, smiled and quickly told his wife to pinch and squeeze the baby rabbits' toes. The Rabbit's children started to scream and cry louder than ever, louder than the Leopard has ever heard them cry. The Rabbit then spoke with a loud voice to be clearly heard by the Leopard and the Baboon,

> "Dear Mrs Rabbit, why are the children crying?"
>
> "They are crying because they want to eat some leopard's liver," Mrs Rabbit answered.
>
> The crafty and cunning Rabbit replied. "I planned with the Baboon that he would bring the Leopard to me, so I could cut his liver. And true to his word the Baboon has.

Keep calm and do not cry, my children. I will get you some leopard's liver right this second."

When the Leopard heard the Rabbit, he became very scared and worried. Unsure, he confronted the Baboon,

"Was this your plan, Mr Baboon? Did you want to betray me? Did you want me to be killed and my liver to be eaten by the Rabbit and his family? You made me believe you were on my side all along! How could you deceive a friend?"

"I swear this was not my plan at all," asserted the Baboon.

"It is the crafty old Rabbit again, trying to trick us both!"

"I do not know who to believe!" replied the Leopard with agitation.

"I think I better eat you right now so that you are unable to take me any further and deliver me to the Rabbit."

The Baboon tried to run away, but he could not because his tail was tied to the Leopard's tail. The Leopard was also trying to escape, but he could not because his tail was tied to the Baboon's. They were pulling each other in opposite directions. Their tails were getting seriously bruised until they stopped pulling to untie them. As soon as they got free, they both took to their heels.

The crafty Rabbit, even though smaller than both the Leopard and the Baboon, was left with the whole house for him, Mrs Rabbit and his baby rabbits.

8

The Two Cold Porcupines

Introduction

The tale of *The Two Cold Porcupines* is an African Folktale from Tanzania, in Eastern Africa. A major landmark of Tanzania is the archipelagos of Zanzibar, a famous World Heritage Site. *Mount Kilimanjaro*, *Lake Tanganyika* or *Kambo Water Falls* are equally well-known sites. Interesting fact, the name Tanzania was created as a clipped compound of the names of the two states that unified to create the country: *Tanganyika* and Zanzibar.

The folktale is about relationships, about the balance between being close to people and allowing them their personal space. The tale is told through animals as an analogy for human beings.

The story has been transmitted orally in *Kaonde*, a Bantu language, and one version was collected in Dar es Salaam by Father Bernard Joinet, a Catholic Priest and founder of the *Fleet of Hope*, an organization fighting AIDS in Tanzania.

The story of *The Two Cold Porcupines* is about two Porcupines who had no shelter from the cold, just each other for body warmth. But, because of their physical make-up, containing sharp spikes, they had to be careful to not cause injury.

The Folktale

The Serengeti National Park in Tanzania has huge empty plains. One cold night two Porcupines found themselves there alone, without any shelter from the harsh elements, and no place where they could keep warm. They only had their own body heat to keep them warm.

> "What can we do for warmth?" asked the first porcupine to the other.
>
> "Well, we could huddle close to one another," answered the second.
>
> "Though I am worried that during the night we could accidentally prick or even kill the other by mistake."

So, after experimenting for some time, and with a few exclamations of

"Ouch!!!!"

They found a convenient distance to stand next to one another. They were close enough so that their bodies gave heat to one another, and helped to keep them warm. But they were far enough apart so that they would not prick one another throughout the night.

So it is too with personal human relationships. In daily life, we have to find the right balance. We need to be close enough together so that we create friendships and are able to share, but not too close to a person so that we become overly intrusive or invasive. People need space to develop and grow and be an individual, whilst having their friends nearby. This is about closeness without being smothering and overbearing. Another way of putting it is that we need proximity with enough distance, it is all about the balance. In Sukuma, Tanzania, there is a proverb that says:

> "Those who love each other, do not tread on each other's toes."

9

The Honey Bird and the Three Gourds

Introduction

The tale of *The Honey Bird and the Three Gourds* is an African Folktale from Zambia, a Southern Africa country surrounded by the lands such as the Democratic Republic of Congo, Tanzania, Malawi, Angola, Zimbabwe, Namibia, Mozambique, and Botswana. The famous *Victoria Falls* waterfall is in the South West forming the border with Zimbabwe.

The story is about some concepts such as death, ageing, evil, good, curiosity and Gods. The Greek Mythology tale of Pandora's Box is a variation of it, for in Pandora's case, she opened a box, and all evils flew into the world.

The folktale may have been relayed multiples times, though the version presented here was collected and relayed in the *Kaonde* language, a Bantu language.

The story of *The Honey Bird and the Three Gourds* is about disobeying a powerful figure of authority, and the consequences for everyone. It is can be understood as a way of instilling a sense of respect for elders.

The Folktale

One day, a God asked Mayimba the Honey Bird to meet with him. The God gave the Mayimba three gourds which were all sealed, and gave the Honey Bird the following instruction,

> "Go to the man and the woman I first created, and give them these three gourds. But, you are not to open them on the way. When you reach their village, you need to relay the message:
>
> 'Open this gourd first, it contains seeds which you will need to plant for food.'
>
> But, tell them not to open the other gourds until I arrive. When I will arrive, I will advise them on what to do with the other two gourds."

Mayimba the Honey Bird started the very long journey to his friends, but he was overwhelmed with curiosity about what the gourds contained. When he could not resist the temptation anymore, he stopped flying and opened the first gourd that contained the seeds. When he saw that this did just contain seeds, he replaced the seeds back into the gourd and closed it once again.

Mayimba the Honey Bird thought about continuing on his journey, but the other gourds were teasing his mind, and he decided to open the second gourd.

The second gourd contained medicine, which had the ability to cure death, illness, tiredness and to tame wild and dangerous animals. But Mayimba had never experienced any of those things, so did not understand what they were, or how valuable they were. Mayimba placed them back into the second gourd and fastened it back up.

Mayimba the Honey Bird thought about just flying ahead with his mission and taking the gourds to his friends as instructed. Yet again, the third and final gourd kept occupying his mind. His curiosity was aroused and he wanted to know what was inside. When he opened the gourd, the container was filled with death, disease and dangerous animals.

When the gourd was opened, everything escaped and was dispersed throughout the world. Mayimba the Honey Bird tried to recapture them but was not able to. He could not bring them back inside the gourd and it remained empty.

The God came along, as promised. He quickly saw that the Honey Bird had opened all the gourds, disobeying all the instructions he had given him. The God was very angry, yet together with Mayimba the Honey Bird he tried to recapture all of the evil spirits and being that the Honey Bird had released.

But they were not able to do so. The God was furious, and

said to Mayimba,

"You have done a very wicked thing! This is your fault."

Mayimba the Honey Bird was frightened when he heard the God disapproval. Therefore, in fear and in tears, he flew into the wilderness wishing to never come back to the village where the first man and the first woman lived.

The God went to visit the first man and the first woman he had created, Mulonga and his wife Mwinambuzhi. They were the first on earth, the first people who Mayimba the Honey Bird was to have given the sealed and unopened gourds to. The God said to them,

> "Your friend Mayimba the Honey Bird has made a serious mistake, by failing to follow my instructions. He was eagerly curious to know what I had prepared for you and he could not wait to open the gourds that I sent you.
>
> He has unknowingly started great trouble for this world, and even I will not be able to repair the damage that he has done.
>
> However, I will teach you how to do useful things, such as sew clothes, build houses. You will be able then to find shelter from the elements and wild creatures.
>
> I will teach you how to make fire by rubbing two dry sticks together, and I will teach you to make tools and weapons such as axes, spears, cooking and water pots."

From this day, Mulonga, Mwinambuzhi, and all their children and descendants had to learn new skills they found they needed in order to eat, survive and flourish. Unfortunately, due to Mayimba's curiosity, their life had also changed and they have now to deal with evils such as diseases, death and wild animals.

10

Ssebwaato the Hero

Introduction

The tale of *Ssebwaato* is an African Folktale from Uganda. Uganda is non-coastal inland East African country, surrounded by Kenya, the Democratic Republic of Congo and South Sudan. The southern part of Uganda is limited by the *Lake Victoria*. *Swahili* is the most widely spoken language in Uganda, with several other languages such as *Runyoro*, *Runyankole*, *Luo* and *Luganda*.

This story is mythical and magical and quite like a fairytale, it is an adventure story where the hero travels with hurdles to overcome along the way and a quest to find a treasure. It is a story about forging friendships.

The folktale has been transmitted over decades, and this particular version was recorded from the *Baganda*, a Bantu tribe. The *Bangada* society is very much hierarchical, driven by social rules and with an awareness for elders and for superiors.

Part of the Uganda culture though carries the firm belief that you can carve out a positive future for yourself by carefully choosing your friends. This is quite relevant to this particular story, where *Ssebwaato*'s friends help him in his journey to success.

The story tells the tale of a man called *Ssebwaato* who goes in search of a cure for his ill leg. He experiences adventures on his way and he makes some good friends for life. He eventually ends up becoming a King.

The Folktale

Once upon a time, there was a man called Ssebwaato, he lived in a village with his wife Lwandeka. Ssebwaato had a poorly leg with a wound on it that just would not heal, regardless of all the remedies he would try on it. His good friend Sserwalilundi recommended that he contact a world-renowned medicine healing Doctor called Nnende.

Ssebwaato went to visit Nnende in his hut, which was full of bottles of potions, and strange objects hanging up containing feathers, beads and bones.

> "I will be able to provide you with the instructions for how to locate a cure.
>
> But before I do this, you need to provide me with a white goat, a white chicken, nine cowrie shells, and a roll of bark cloth.
>
> When you bring me these, I will help you," said Nnende the medicine man.

Ssebwaato went off, gathered these items right in his village and returned to Nnende. The medicine man gave Ssebwaato the instructions, and also advised him to request his wife and children to make him a basket of grilled corn, a basket of roasted peanuts, and a basket of sesame seeds called sim sim. Ssebwaato's family obliged, and he set off on his journey. He intended to travel to a distant land where there were Giant-sized people-eating Chimpanzees. It was in this land, where Ssebwaato would find the cure for his leg wound.

On his journey, Ssebwaato met Wammese (also known as Mr Rat). The two made a friendship pact, and Mr Rat offered Ssebwato two gourds which he had filled with water.

The next person Ssebwaato met on his journey was Nabbubi (also known as Mr Spider), and he made a friendship pact with him too. Soon on the journey, Ssebwaato reached a huge lake, but there were no boats to be seen to allow him to make his way across it. He needed to cross the lake to reach the land where the Giant man-eating Chimpanzees lived. He called out to his friend Mr Spider,

> "Mr Spider, as part of our friendship pact, are you able to help me cross the lake?"
>
> "Yes, I can create a web of threads, which you can then

use as a zip-wire to travel across the water to the land of the Giant man-eating Chimpanzees."

Nabbubi did this, Ssebwaato did that and glided over the lake to arrive in the land of the Giant man-eating Chimpanzees. The land of the Chimpanzees looked like a ghost town, everything was eerily quiet, and all that Ssebwaato could see were masses of human skulls and just one solitary hut. A lady's voice called out from the hut. When Ssebwaato entered, he found an elderly woman who had been already half-eaten by the Chimpanzees. Ssebwaato explained his quest to find a cure, to what the lady said,

> "The medicine you require is inside this very hut. It is hidden inside that drum there hung up above the hearth. But, as you will know, this hut is heavily guarded. My advice to you is to steal the drum when the Giant man-eating Chimpanzees are back and have fallen asleep."

It soon became night-time, and the old woman could hear the Giant man-eating Chimpanzees returning. The lady told Ssebwaato to hide underneath a massive saucepan. When the Giant Chimpanzees came in, they were highly suspicious because they could smell human flesh.

> "I have not seen a single human being," the elderly lady insisted, lying.

The Chimpanzees fell asleep, and the elderly lady tapped gently against the huge saucepan, to indicate to Ssebwaato that it was safe to come out. Ssebwaato crept out, and wasted no time, he cut the drum loose from above the hearth, but he was horrified at the fact, that the drum started beating a rhythm all of its own. The drum was able to beat out the words:

> "I have gone."

The sound of the drum beating out the words woke up the Giant man-eating Chimpanzees. They saw that Ssebwaato had taken the drum, and they started to chase after him to retrieve it. As they drew closer to him, Ssebwaato decided to use some of the food that his family had packed him up with. He tipped some of the roasted peanuts on the ground behind him. The greedy Giant Chimpanzees were excited to find the roast peanuts and stopped to eat them, whilst Ssebwaato was able to put more distance between himself and the Chimpanzees. Each time after, when the Chimpanzees started gaining on him, Ssebwaato would put some more of the food that his family had packed him up with, onto the ground: roasted peanuts, grilled corn or sesame seeds.

The food did not last forever though, and Ssebwaato ran out of food to give to the Giant Chimpanzees and once again they were getting dangerously close to him. It was at this point that Ssebwaato remembered his friend Wammese also known as Mr Rat. Ssebwaato called out to Mr Rat, who came scurrying along. Mr Rat said to Ssebwaato,

> "Remember those two gourds of water? Pour out their contents."

Even though the gourds were small, they had magical properties. Water flowed and flowed out of them. Until there was enough water to create an entire lake. This lake separated Ssebwaato from the Giant man-eating Chimpanzees. The Chimpanzees lamented,

> "You have taken wealth, you have taken goats, you have taken cows, you have taken wives..."

Ssebwaato did not really know what they were referring to, nor did he care.

However, he journeyed back home, taking the magical drum

with him. Immediately upon arriving back in his home village, the drum stopped beating its rhythm. The entire village had gathered to meet Ssebwaato and welcome him back home. Ssebwaato placed a hunting knife into the drum, intending to find the medicine to cure his leg. However, when he did this, suddenly lot and lots of humans and animals started to come out of the drum: women, men, children, cows, goats, everything that the Giant man-eating Chimpanzees had ever eaten.

In the final corner of the drum, Ssebwaato found the medicine. He unscrewed the lid, scooped out the cream and applied it to his leg. His wound was cured instantly, and he would walk again without any pain.

Ssebwaato became known to everyone and founded a new nation. He was made King of all the people who he had resurrected from the drum.

11

Why the Chicken Hawk Eats Chickens

Introduction

The tale of *Why the Chicken Hawk Eats Chickens* is an African Folktale from Kenya, notably from the *Kamba* people a Bantu group mostly situated in the lowlands of Kenya.

Mythology is an important part of every culture and family is a vital part of the *Kamba* community, with children being welcome at all houses.

The folktale uses animals in order to impart a moral lesson to society, about death, healing, self-sacrifice and sin. It is a story that gives an explanation for why things happen in nature. The love between parents and children and the desire for revenge upon a child's death is at the core of this folktale.

This version of the story has been relayed by the *Kamba* people and collected by Dr John M. in Kenya.

The story tells the tale of a mother chicken hawk with an ill child. She seeks medicine for her child from a spider who himself gets eaten by a hen.

The Folktale

There once was a very young Chicken Hawk who was also very sick. A man spoke to the Mother Chicken Hawk and said,

> "I know of a medicine-man Spider who has the ability to cure your child. You need to give me fifty thousand gold coins, then I will go and fetch the medicine-man Spider for you."

Even though it was all her life's savings, the Mother Chicken Hawk's love for her child meant that she happily parted with the money. She would have done anything, to keep her child alive. She was delighted at the thought of a cure. The mother gave the man the fifty thousand coins and he went away to fetch the medicine-man Spider. The man reached the Spider, and said to him,

> "Spider! Spider! Oh, will not you please come quickly and help us. The Mother Chicken Hawk has a very

poorly baby, and she has asked me to come and fetch you so that you can cure the baby. Will you come now?"

"Your Hen saw me yesterday, and threatened to eat me if she sees me again! I am tiny in comparison to the Hen. If I go alone, there is a real risk that I will be eaten!"

But, the man was busy and was unable to accompany the Spider. Yet he insisted that it was important for him to go alone, without him.

The Spider gathered up all the medicine bottles that he thought he would need, and placed them into a bag which he carried on his shoulders. He went alone, as the man would not accompany him, but was very hesitant, unhappy, and worried. He knew that he was at a high risk of being eaten before he even got to the Chicken Hawk's house.

The Spider turned a corner and spotted the Hen. He scuttled off to the side of the road and hid near the path. But, the quick-eyed Hen had seen the movement and spotted the Spider. She picked him up with her beak and placed the Spider in the nest for her chicks to eat. The Spider quickly managed to scrawl a note to his family, and left his medicine bottles there, before he died.

The Chicken Hawk mother, with the ill child, waited and waited for the Medicine-man Spider to arrive, but he never did.

"Where is he? I wonder when he will get here?" said the Mother Chicken Hawk.

Eventually, out of despair, she went out to look for him, in case he had gotten lost. She did not know he had been eaten. She found the broken medicine bottles, and a letter addressed to her. She picked it up, opened it, and read:

"To the Chicken Hawk Mother, I was on my way to your

home to treat your baby, but I met the Mother Hen, who took me and gave me to her chicks to eat."

The Mother Chicken Hawk, flew back to her nest after she read the letter. She felt helpless that she was unable to help her child. A few days later the baby Chicken Hawk died. The mother suffered so much grief, that only a mother who has lost her child can understand. She decided to take revenge on hens, and from that day onwards, she began to eat chickens.

This is why today you will see the Mother Chicken Hawk, catching chicks and flying away with them, to eat them. She passed a law for the rest of the birds and human beings, that they should also eat hens' chicks and adult chickens. Even to this day, if you catch a Hen, it says,

"It is not I! It is not I!"

The Hen means that it was not her, who killed the Spider, who was on his way to cure the baby Chicken Hawk.

12

They Quickly Came with Love and Concern

Introduction

The tale of *They Quickly Came with Love and Concern* is an African Folktale from Kenya.

This story comes from the *Gusii* people, also known as the *Kisii* or *AbaGusii*. It is a Bantu subgroup who lives in two parts of

Western Kenya. The mythology around this group is that people from this tribe are resilient, hard-working and of tough nature.

The folktale is about love, relationships, families and people's real nature.

This folktale may have been relayed many times over the years, but this version was collected by Evans, Ny, in Gusii, Kenya.

The story tells the tale of a generous man, who has many friends whilst he is generous. But, when he is in need, he has to find who is truly there for him.

The Folktale

Once upon a time, a Man had experienced disagreements with his brothers and sisters over land and was unhappy there. So, he left his home and his village and instead moved in with his Wife's relatives. In his Wife's relatives' village, he worked incredibly hard to forge a new life for himself there. He did very well. He became wealthy and was in a position to purchase a great deal of land and many properties. He built the largest house in the village.

He was a kind and considerate man, who was very generous to the relatives he had lived with and with the entire village. If any villager had an issue, he would invite them into his house and help them. Whenever there was a party or celebration or typical holiday he would invite all the villagers to his house to celebrate the event with him. All the villagers thought that he was wonderful, and kind, and praised him for how generous he was, helping all who needed it.

One day, the Man said to his Wife,

"I think that my relatives here, and everyone in this

entire village only love me because of my generosity."

His Wife disagreed because she wanted her family to think that everyone loved her husband for who he was.

The Man, however, felt as though his Wife was simply deluding herself. He had seen for himself how people truly treated him. He had worked hard, to make his money, but his relatives and all the villagers seemed bothered by his wealth – he could tell by the way that they made snide allusions to it from time to time, or about his house, or the clothes his Wife wore – but he had worked hard to get there and live the way he did. The majority of the villagers though were lazy and had not worked as hard as him throughout their life. But somehow they felt that Life owed them something.

With his Wife, the Man elaborated a plan to demonstrate to his Wife, all the things he had observed about the people where they currently lived. He hoped that by showing his Wife their true nature, she would then fully believe him, and they would return to their previous village.

So, the Man pretended to be ill. Very few of the villagers were truly bothered enough about him to come and visit, which demonstrated their lack of care and concern for him. They were fair-weather friends and only there when things were good with him, and when he could be of benefit to them.

Then, the Man found a mongoose that had died of natural causes, and he wrapped its body, which was starting to decompose in a blanket, and placed it under his bed. The stench that came from the rotting mongoose was horrendous, it made him and his Wife, almost retch at the stink. The Man asked his Wife to scream loudly and pretend that her husband had died in bed. His Wife's relatives and the villagers came at the sound of her screams and gathered in the home to ask about it. None of them was willing to go into the bedroom to confirm the death, because of the awful smell coming from the mongoose. His Wife's relatives, and the villagers, soon would only stand at the doorway of the house, but would not enter any further.

When the message reached his brothers and sisters, they quickly came with love and concern, and they went straight to the bed, regardless of the stench emanating from it. They immediately realised that their brother was not there, and discovered that the smell was coming from the rotten mongoose, that had been wrapped in a blanket and placed under his bed. It was at that moment, that the Man came out of hiding, and he welcomed his brothers and sisters with open arms. They were incredibly relieved to see that he was still alive, and enveloped him in a hug.

After that, he decided to hold a large party where he fed his family well, the ones who had not been put off by the smell. They had come out of love and concern, and not for reasons of greed, or false-entitlement. The Man and his Wife decided to move back to their original village to be closer to his family, who were always there for him and loved him no matter what.

13

The Jackal and the Spring

Introduction

The tale of *The Jackal and the Spring* is an African Folktale from South Africa. The South African coast is bathed both by the Atlantic Ocean and by the Indian Ocean. Some landmarks include the *Kruger National Park*, and the *Drakensberg*, an escarpment that stretches for over 600 miles from the Eastern Cape Province in the South, then successively forms, in order from south to north, the border between Lesotho and the Eastern Cape and the border between Lesotho and KwaZulu-Natal Province.

There is a definite folktale structure to this three-part story. There are three incidents, the first two times the scenario plays out pretty similarly. But something different happens the third time.

The folktale describes laziness, cunning, gullibility, naivety, unfairness, team-work, diligence and steadfastness.

The story may have been relayed many times over the years, but this one version was collected by E. Jacotted in *Contes Populaires des Bassoutos*. Andrew Lang then included it in his *The Grey Fairy* Book.

The story of *The Jackal and the Spring* is about a cunning Jackal, a foolish rabbit, a foolish hare, and a clever tortoise.

The Folktale

Once upon a time all the streams and riverbeds, were completely parched and dry, with just brown cracked and crumbling mud. The animals began to panic that they would die of thirst, as they did not know where they could fetch water from. They searched the local area, and eventually found a small spring. However, they needed to dig it deeper to ensure they would have access to plenty of water. The animals said to one another,

> "Let us create a well because then we will not spend all our time worrying that we will die of thirst."

All of the animals agreed, with the exception of the Jackal. The Jackal was very lazy, with a superior lofty attitude, he detested doing any kind of work, and wherever he could, he would get others to do it for him.

When the animals had finished digging the well, they held a meeting to decide who should be made *Guardian of the Well*. They did not want the Jackal to benefit from the water, because he had not helped to create the well.

> "He would not work, therefore he shall not drink!" the animals protested.

After a discussion had taken place, it was decided that the Rabbit would be the *Guardian of the Well*. Therefore, the Rabbit went to the well and settled down, and the other animals returned to their homes.

When the other animals had gone, and it was just the Rabbit on his own; the crafty devious Jackal approached.

> "Good morning! Good morning, Rabbit!" shouted the Jackal.

> "Good Morning," the Rabbit politely replied.

The Jackal then took out a bag that hung at his side, opened it, and withdrew a piece of honeycomb. He began to eat it, with a rapturous look on his face. He turned to the Rabbit and said,

> "As you see, Rabbit, I am not thirsty in the least, and this is much nicer than any water."

> "Would you please let me try a bit?" begged the Rabbit, salivating.

The Jackal snapped off a tiny morsel of the honeycomb and handed it to him.

> "Oh my goodness, that is amazing!" said the Rabbit in ecstasy.

"Could I please have a little bit more, dear Jackal?"

"If you really want some more of the honeycomb, you must have your paws tied behind your back and then you lay on your back so that I can pour the honeycomb into your mouth," answered the astute Jackal.

The Rabbit was fantasizing with greed of the Jackal's delicious honeycomb because it was so sweet and tasty, he thought he would do anything for it. Therefore, he did as the Jackal asked. He let the Jackal tie his paws tightly behind his back, and place him on his back staring up at the sky.

The honeycomb never came. Instead, the Jackal ran to the spring that the other animals had taken the time to make into a large well, and he drank and drank water until he was satiated. The Jackal then returned to his den and left the Rabbit laying there prone.

In the evening, the animals returned and they saw the Rabbit laying on his back with his paws tied. They said to him,

"Rabbit, how did you let yourself be deceived by the Jackal like this?"

"It is the Jackal's fault!" protested the Rabbit, "He tied me up with my paws behind my back and promised me some delicious honeycomb. It was all a crafty plan, just so that he could drink our water."

"Rabbit, you are no better than an idiot, to allow the Jackal the opportunity to drink our water, when he would not help to create the well. Who will be our next watchman? We must have someone sharper than the Rabbit," retorted the animals disapprovingly.

There was a little Hare in the crowd. "I will be the

watchman," he told the audience.

That evening the animals went off to their homes and left the little Hare to guard the spring. After they had left, it was the early hours of the morning, the Jackal approached.

"Good morning! Good morning little Hare," said the Jackal.

"Good morning Jackal," replied the little Hare.

"Could you give me some tobacco?" politely asked the Jackal.

"I am sorry, but I do not have any," answered the little Hare.

The Jackal then sat down next to the little Hare, took out his bag, and pulled out of it a piece of delicious honeycomb. He popped it in his mouth, rolled his eyes upwards in delight and exclaimed,

"Oh, little Hare, if you only knew how good this tastes!"

"What is it?" asked the little Hare.

"It is something that makes my mouth lovely and refreshed and hydrated," answered the cunning Jackal.

"So that after I have eaten it, I no longer feel thirsty. I am sure, that you and the other animals, forever want water?"

"Please, would you let me have a little bit?" begged the little Hare.

"Not so fast," replied the Jackal.

"If you really want to savour every mouthful and enjoy what you are eating, you must have your paws tied behind your, lay on your back, so that I can pour the delicious honeycomb into your mouth."

"Ok, I will agree, on the condition that we do this quickly!" pressed the little Hare.

The Jackal tied the Hare's paws tightly and laid him on the back. The honeycomb never arrived, and instead, the Jackal went down the well, and drank and drank and drank from it, until he was full of water. When he finished, the Jackal returned to his den.

In the evening all the animals returned. They saw the little Hare with his paws behind his back, and they said to him,

"Little Hare, how did you let yourself be taken in by the Jackal? You know the very same thing happened to the Rabbit. Did not you boast that you were very sharp? You undertook to guard our water in the well, but the Jackal has been drinking it again! How much is left for us?"

"It is the Jackal's fault," replied the little Hare.

"He told me he would give me some of his delicious honeycomb if I agreed to let him tie my paws behind my back."

The animals were very disappointed with the Rabbits and the Hare's foolishness.

"Who can we trust to guard our Spring and Well now?" they asked.

After some discussion, the Panther reached the conclusion,

"Let it be the Tortoise."

The animals went off to their homes, leaving the Tortoise to guard the well. As soon as they had gone, the Jackal appeared.

"Good morning Tortoise, Good morning," began the Jackal.

But the Tortoise deliberately chose to ignore him and did not answer.

"Good morning Tortoise, Good morning," The Jackal said once again.

But again, the Tortoise carried on as though he was completely oblivious to the Jackal having spoken. The Jackal could not believe his luck. He thought to himself,

"The animals have replaced the Rabbit, and the Hare, with an even more foolish animal. I shall simply just kick him to one side, and go and have a drink!"

So, the Jackal went up to the Tortoise, and said to him in a soft voice,

"Tortoise! Tortoise!"

But, the Tortoise once again blanked him. The Jackal kicked the Tortoise out of the way, and went to the well, and began to drink the cool water. However, scarcely had his mouth touched the water when he felt a firm grip around his leg. He quickly lifted his head out of the well, to see what was going on. The Tortoise had seized him firmly by the leg. The Jackal cried out loudly,

"Ow!!!! Stop! You will break my leg!"

But the Tortoise continued to hold on tightly. The Jackal managed to take out his bag that contained the honeycomb and tried to get the Tortoise to smell it, to tempt him. But, the Tortoise very deliberately turned his head away so that he could not smell anything. The Jackal who was getting desperate by this stage, usually his honeycomb was enough to tempt pretty much anyone, said,

> "Look, if you will let go of my leg, I will give you this bag, and its content – all the delicious honeycomb!"

The Tortoise did not give any verbal reply, but just gripped the Jackal's leg tighter. He managed to keep the Jackal pinned in such a way until all the other animals returned. On seeing all the other animals gathered around, the Jackal was very scared as he did not know what he would do if they all attacked him. So, he gave a violent tug, managed to free his leg from the Tortoise's grip, and then scarpered away from the animals as fast as he could. All the animals praised the Tortoise and the Panther said,

> "Well done, Tortoise! You have proved you are both wise and courageous. You did not fall for the Jackal's tricks, and you were brave and strong enough to prevent him from drinking the water. Now we can all drink from our well in peace, as you have outwitted the thieving Jackal!"

14

A Man, A Bird and Ogres

Introduction

The tale of *A Man, A Bird and Ogres* is an African Folktale from Tanzania. Due to the country being bathed by the Indian Ocean, with its semi-autonomous region the archipelago of Zanzibar, there are lots of marine spots. One of them is the *Menai Bay Conservation Area*, the largest protected marine area in the region.

This story comes from the *Sukuma* people, a Bantu subgroup and the largest ethnic group in Tanzania. The word *Sukuma* means North, where the *Sukuma* people live. They believe in spirit possession and have a holistic lens of viewing the world as interconnected with all living things, natural and supernatural. This is particularly significant for this folk-tale.

This version of the folktale was collected by Sister Immaculate Mirambo. Sister Immaculate Mirambo belongs to the *Sisters of Our Lady Queen of the Apostles of Mbeya* and has done a lot of work on the oral culture of the *Sukuma* people.

This folktale is about helping the needy, and altruism. It is also about being grateful. The story tells the tale of a kind man, who helps a poorly bird, later in his life, the same bird looks out for him and helps him.

The Folktale

Once upon a time, a man who was called Magulu Abili (also known as *Two Legs*) went into a forest and started to cut down trees, in order to build himself a house.

Whilst he was doing this, he noticed a little bird that was sat on the forest floor, looking very poorly. The little bird was so weak at this point it was no longer able to get food or water for itself. He got a little container and poured some water into it, and took to the bird some grain. The bird was so thankful for this sustenance. The man also scooped the little bird up and took it home, so that it could fully recover from its illness, in safety away from any dangerous predators.

The little bird made a full recovery and it was soon the day where Magulu Abili was able to pick the bird up, take her to the window, and set her free to fly and go about her business. She was very grateful for all his help, and said to him,

"One day, I will help you too."

If Magulu was being honest, he did not really think that such a tiny little bird, would ever be able to help him, a fully-grown man, in the future. But, he said thank you and waved the bird goodbye, never truly expecting to see her again.

Days and weeks later, Magulu Abili was working in the forest cutting down some more timber, and he came across some Ogres. He tried to hide, but as soon as they set their eyes on him, they started chasing him, with the intention of killing him and making a sumptuous meal without any doubt.

Magulu looked around wildly trying to find someplace to hide. He was solely surrounded by trees. He decided to try and climb a tree, to hide out of the Ogres reach. Whilst Magulu was just shimmying up the tree, he noticed that the Ogres had stopped dead in their tracks and were looking skyward, distracted by something. The bird that Magulu had helped was fluttering around the heads of the ogres moving from tree to tree singing a tune. The Ogres were focussed upon this bird and swiped at it with their large and clumsy hands. But the bird was much too quick for the Ogres. The bird gradually led the Ogres further away from where Magulu had climbed the tree.

Magulu was eventually able to climb back down the tree because the Ogres were much further away now. As soon as he landed on the ground, he took to his heels back home. He was so thankful to the bird who had saved him. He remembered the bird that was ill at his house and how he had helped her, and he knew immediately that it was the very same bird that he had saved, who had come back to fulfil her promise of returning the help.

15

A Stubborn Person Sails in a Clay Boat

Introduction

The tale of *A Stubborn Person Sails in a Clay Boat* is an African Folktale from Tanzania. The specific town where this folktale is taken from is Bukoba in Northwest Tanzania, on the western shore of *Lake Victoria*. The city, surrounded by hills, has a beautiful white sandy beach, and a large market.

The story may have been relayed several times, but this version of the tale was collected by Sister Rita Ishengoma in Bukoba. She has worked on providing retreats to novices of her congregation and was active sharing Bibles in small Christian communities.

This folktale is about obedience and punishment. It narrates the story of a disobedient daughter-in-law who ignored the advice of her mother-in-law and suffered the consequences.

The Folktale

One day in Western Tanzania, in the Kagera Region a man married a beautiful lady. Her mother-in-law spent time teaching her the customs and traditions that had been passed down through generations of the family.

After some time, the mother-in-law took her daughter-in-law to a secret part of the house and showed her a large pot which was fixed firmly in place, with a huge sturdy lid.

> "You must never open this pot, never even go near this pot, never touch it," said the mother-in-law.
>
> "Do you understand?"
>
> "Yes, Mama, I do," replied the daughter in law.

The pot appeared to have magical powers. The daughter-in-law was astonished when one day she saw the pot fill itself with water, at the mother-in-law's command. The family never had to go and fetch heavy pots of water from the lake, which was a daily routine that all the other villagers had to do.

One day the mother-in-law had been away all day, visiting family in a distant village. She was late to return home. There was no water available in the house, whilst water is essential to cook. The daughter-in-law thought to herself,

> "Why can not I use the pot, and get it to fill with water as my mother-in-law does?"

She thought about this some more and thought,

> "What harm could it do, if I was just to open the lid of the pot and look inside?"

She pushed aside in her mind all the previous warnings that her mother-in-law had given her, and bravely decided to pursue her own route of action.

The daughter-in-law went to the secret place in the house, to fetch the heavy magical pot. As soon as she touched the pot, it shattered into millions of pieces. Water began to pour from the pot, and would not stop! The daughter-in-law called out,

> "Mulanjuna! Mulanjuna!"

Which meant,

> "Help! Help!"

But, nobody came to her assistance. The water got higher and higher and the daughter-in-law could no longer breathe.

The mother in-law was a witch, and she knew through her magic powers that someone had touched her pot that was fixed in the secret place of her house. She hurried back home immediately. On arriving at home, she saw the water flowing from out of the large magical pot. She took out from her purse her magical hoe, made from skin, that she always carried. Holding the hoe out towards the flood, she shouted,

> "Oitke Akalo Osige Akandi! Oite Abalo Osige Abandi!"

This meant,

"Kill one and spare the others!"

The disobedient daughter-in-law had already drowned by this time, the entire house and all the land surrounding were flooded. The mother in law planted the magical hoe into the ground, and that stopped any further water.

All the people from the surrounding village gathered to look at the new lake that had appeared. They decided to call the lake

"Ikimba".

There is the Haya proverb:

"Entagambirwa esabala bw'aibumba"

Which means,

"A stubborn person sails in a clay boat"

This means that if a person stubbornly does not change his views, and goes ahead with actions out of stubbornness, he would soon sink, as though he was attempting to sail in a clay boat, be in water too deep to stand in and drown.

Every time someone passed by Lake Ikimba, they would remember the daughter-in-law who was stubborn and disobedient and was killed by the magic pot.

16

Changing the Face of the Mountain

Introduction

The tale of *Changing the Face of the Mountain* is an African Folktale from Nairobi, Kenya's capital and largest city. The Maasai name Nairobi means *cool water* as the Nairobi river run throughout the city.

The folktale is about nature, environment, faith, patience, life, and creation.

This version of the story was collected by Sister Joan Marie, and Sister Carolyn Masicha both from the *School Sisters of Notre Dame* which focuses on educating, providing vocational training, healthcare, and spiritual support to women and HIV/AIDs victims in Africa.

The story tells the tale of a wise old lady who made a difference to the future generations by her daily actions.

The Folktale

Once upon a time, in a village called Kamamusa, located in Kenya, a village that was not known for its friendliness, there lived an elderly lady called Bibi Tumaini. The village was situated at the side of a mountain. All of Bibi's neighbours thought she was a strange old lady, with bizarre habits.

On the mountain it was cold and frosty outside, so most of the villagers stayed indoors in front of their fireplaces, trying to keep warm. They were not very sociable or hospitable, and most people only made time to speak to their immediate family.

Even when the weather was less cold, not many people ventured to the mountainside, because it was grey and bleak. It tended to be only children who climbed the mountain in secret, as an act of petulance, because their parents had forbidden them to do so.

Many children in their games of adventure and exploration, had met Bibi. Usually, she was bent over, digging a hole in the ground, and dropping a tiny something into it. The braver of the children would often say,

"Granny, what are you doing?"

Her mysterious reply was always the same,

"I am changing the face of the mountain."

Over time the children grew up and left the village to work in the big nearby city. One of these children had grown into a beautiful lady called Mazingira. She had moved away like others, got married and had children of her own. Yet one day, she wanted to show to her husband and children the village from where she was from, she wanted them to see the harsh environment of bleak mountains where she grew up.

However, when Mazingira returned to Kamamusa, she did not recognize the place where she had spent years of her childhood climbing the forbidden mountain. Instead of bleak sheer cliffs, the entire mountainside was covered with a beautiful array of every colour known to man and every kind of flower you could ever imagine. The flowers gently swayed in the breeze and looked wonderful.

There were vivid coloured bushes with striking variegated leaves, glossy green ferns and even young trees that gave some protection to the many children and adults at the foot of the mountain. All the flowers and the trees had truly brought the mountain and its people to life. Families and neighbours gathered and had parties together. There was such a greater sense of community, as everyone helped one another, chatted with each other, laughed and played games.

Mazinga, who had returned with her family, stopped one of the villagers and asked,

> "When did all this come about? What happened to the unwelcoming, cold and stark mountainside of my

childhood?"

The villager replied,

> "Do you remember the strange old lady, Bibi Tumaini who lived here? The lady who would wander up and down the mountainside, in all weather, and would dig holes in the soil? It was her who went out every single day, in order to sow seeds. She believed that her hard work would pay off, and look at the the results!"

Mazingira remembered the old and bent lady from her childhood, and she remembered too the answer the lady gave, each time she was asked what she was doing. The lady was old and wise, and determined. She foresaw a better future and worked to create it. One person can really make a huge difference! Each time the lady had been asked what she was doing, she would reply: "I am changing the face of the mountain" and she did. Not just physically with the flowers, but she changed the villagers who lived on the mountain too, making the place much kinder and caring. Mazingira finally understood the meaning of Bibi's words.

17

The Dance for Water or the Rabbit's Triumph

Introduction

The tale of *The Dance for Water or the Rabbit is Triumph* is an African Folktale from South Africa.

This folktale is about team-work, self-entitlement, punishment, and deviousness. The tale is about animals, but morals can be passed on to humans. The rabbit in this folktale appears to be a real prankster, he is always coming out on top and defeats the odds.

This version of the story was collected by James A. Honey, an author interested in South African tales. The story is similar to the *Jackal and the Spring* tale.

The story of *The Dance for Water or the Rabbit is Triumph* is about animals working together as a group in a time of need to help one another. It shows how a person in a group is punished when he is deliberately unhelpful. It is also a story about the rabbit is trickery and quick thinking.

The Folktale

There had been a terrible drought in South Africa, with intense heat that had dried up the rivers, streams and springs, until there was no water anywhere. The animals wandered far and wide in search of water, but could not find any. Nowhere was water freely flowing.

The animals held a meeting, and all of the large animals attended, the Elephant, the Lion, the Tiger, the Jackal and the Wolf, plus the small animals too.

"What should we do?" asked the animals.

A few animals made some suggestions, and these were passed back and forth amongst the group. None of the suggestions seemed viable. Finally, the Jackal said,

> "I have an idea, let all of us go to the dry river bed, and dance; by the weight of us all trampling on the ground, we will tread out the water."

All of the animals thought this was a splendid idea, and everyone was ready to get started instantly, as all were very thirsty and in need of a drink. The Rabbit, however, was scornful and dismissive of their plan. He said arrogantly,

> "I have no intention of going and dancing! All of you are crazy, to think that you will get water from the ground by dancing!"

The other animals took no notice of the sour and untrusting rabbit. They danced and danced, and the water did rise to the surface. They were all enormously pleased, and each animal drank as much water as they could. Because Rabbit did not dance with them, it was decided that he would not be allowed to drink. Rabbit laughed at them scornfully and cheekily with defiance said,

> "I will nevertheless, drink some of the water."

That evening, the Rabbit took a leisurely walk down to the river bed, where all the other animals had danced furiously for a long time. He drank and drank from the river until he had had enough. The following morning, the animals saw his footprints in the mud, and all muttered to themselves that he should not drink when he would not help in raising the water. The Rabbit taunted them, by shouting,

> "Aha! See, I did have some of the water! It was so cool and refreshing and tasted delicious!"

The animals called a meeting. They wondered what they could do, and how they could get hold of the Rabbit. Some animals suggested one method, others suggested another. Finally, the old Tortoise moved forward and said,

> "I will catch the Rabbit?"

The other animals were a bit puzzled by this, because the Tortoise was one of the slowest creatures around, and certainly not up to the speed of the rabbit.

"How will you catch the Rabbit, by yourself?"

Tortoise replied, "I will rub my shell with a pitch, which is black and sticky. I will then go near the edge of the water and lay down. To the Rabbit, I will resemble nothing more than a stone. When Rabbit steps onto my back, his feet will stick fast."

The other animals had to agree this was a clever cunning plan.

"Yes, this is a great idea," they agreed in unison.

After a while, the Tortoise had smothered his shell with a pitch and had slowly step by step made his way down to the river bank. He laid down as he had suggested, and pulled his head into his shell so that he looked like just a round stone.

That evening, the Rabbit arrived and had gone to the water to get a drink.

"Ha!" he laughed to himself sarcastically.

"They are quite decent. They have placed a stone here so that I do not need to get my feet wet."

The Rabbit stood with his left foot on the stone, it stuck fast. The Tortoise then popped his head out.

"Ha! Old Tortoise! It is you that has tricked me, and is holding me by one foot. But, I have another foot here to give you a good kick with."

The Rabbit, did what he said, and kicked the Tortoise with all his might, but it stuck fast to the black sticky pitch on the

Tortoises shell, so now he was held there by his two feet.

"I still have my hind feet, and I will kick you with them!" threatened the Rabbit menacingly.

The Rabbit kicked with all his might, that also stayed stuck on the Tortoises shell where it had made contact.

"Still another foot remains," said the Rabbit adamantly. "I shall stomp on you!"

The Rabbit stomped his final foot on the Tortoise and became even more stuck. The Rabbit tried to use his head to head-butt the Tortoise, and his tail to whip him. But both became stuck fast.

The Tortoise slowly turned himself around, and step-by-step headed back towards the other animals, with the Rabbit stuck fast on his back.

"Ha! Rabbit! This will teach you to be so insolent!" shouted the other animals.

The animals tried to decide the Rabbit is fate. They decided that he should be killed, but could not decide how. They were discussing this in the Rabbit is presence. The cunning rodent started to scream,

"Please do not give me a shameful death!"

"What would be a shameful death?" they asked.

"Please do not take me by the tail, and dash my head against a stone. Please, I beg you do not do this."

It was decided by the animals that a fitting punishment for the Rabbit, would be to do exactly what he had asked them not to. Therefore, they decided that the Rabbit would be taken by his tail, and his head dashed against a stone. What they could not yet decide, was who would do this. The animals decided that the Lion should because he was the strongest.

The Lion walked to the front of the group, and the poor Rabbit was brought to him. The Rabbit begged and pleaded that he did not want to die such a terrible death. The Lion took the Rabbit firmly by the tail and started to swing him around. A white fluffy skin slipped off from the Rabbit's bottom, and the Lion stood there clutching the tail in his paw. The Rabbit wounded but free, his tail fur would soon grow back with time.

18

How the Monkeys Saved the Fish

Introduction

The tale of *How the Monkeys Saved the Fish* is an African Folktale from Tanzania.

This story has been relayed orally over the years, and unfortunately, I could not find who captured it on writing for the first time, likely to be missionaries.

This folktale is about nature and helping the needy, it is also a critique of society where the message is to not meddle with things you know nothing about. It is a tale of good intentions, wrapped in foolishness and lack of understanding.

The story tells the tale of caring, but foolish monkeys who try to assist fish, by assuming the fish are just like them, instead of appreciating their difference and letting the fish govern themselves. The monkeys meant well but ultimately led to the fish demise.

The Folktale

It had reached the end of the monsoon season, and all the ground was flooded from where rivers had overflowed. Never had anyone seen such a downpour and so much water. Most of the animals had run up to drier grounds in the hills, those who had been lucky enough to escape. The floods were so ferocious that some animals had sadly drowned.

The monkeys, because of their nimbleness and ability to climb trees and leap from branch to branch, were safe. They had climbed high up into the branches, and they looked down on the flooded plains and saw fish of beautiful colours swimming in the water below. The monkeys had never seen fish before and had no idea what they were. To the monkeys, they simply looked like legless creatures. The fish swam gracefully and leapt in and out of the water in delight at having such a large playground to swim in. The fish seemed to be the only creatures enjoying the flood, which had pretty much devastated everywhere else.

One of the monkeys saw the fish, which he thought was struggling to breathe in the water and was leaping with the intent to get out, or that he was unable to escape its currents. The monkey said to his friend,

> "Look down, my friend, look at those poor creatures below. They will drown in the water. Cannot you see them struggling?"

"Yes," replied the other monkey.

> "What a shame. They were probably unable to run up the hills when the floodwater came so quickly because they do not appear to have any legs. Do you think we can save them?"

> "I think we should definitely try. Let us climb down the trees, and stand near the edge. There we can reach into the water, but the water will not cover us, or sweep us away. From our vantage point, we should be able to help them get out of the water."

So, that is exactly what the monkeys did. It was really hard work, trying to scoop the fish out of the water, without losing their footing, and overbalancing into the water themselves, they had to be very careful. But, gradually, one by one, they scooped the fish up and placed them onto the dry land.

After a while, there was quite a large pile of fish laying on the grass, all completely still, not moving at all. One of the monkeys said to the other,

> "Do you see? They were completely exhausted from trying to stay afloat in the water, and not drown. Now, they are having a good sleep and relaxing. If it had not been for us, my friend, these poor unfortunate creatures with no legs, would definitely have drowned and died."

The other monkey replied,

> "They were trying to get away from us and avoid being

helped out of the water because they did not understand that we only meant well for them. They probably thought we may have caught them and eaten them as predators. However, when they wake up, I am sure they will be grateful then because we brought them salvation, we saved them!"

Both monkeys were completely oblivious to the fact they had caused the fish to die by removing them from the water they needed to live. They only saw the situation from their own perspective. They viewed the flood as bad, and so could not see how the floodwater would actually be pleasurable to the fish. They did not understand that fish were in their element, happy and content. Through lack of knowledge and lack of communication, regardless of their good intentions, both monkeys caused the death of innocent fish.

19

I am the Dancing Man

Introduction

The tale of *I am the Dancing Man* is an African Folktale from Zambia. The story is set in the market town of Lukulu in Western Province. The major ethnic group is *Lozi*, with a subdivision in twenty-four subgroups.

This folktale is about life, vivacity, bringing joy, passing on traditions, and doing good.

The story has been relayed over the years, and this version was captured by Brother Carmine, from *the Santa Maria Mission* in Northern Zambia.

The tale is about a Dancing Man, who spreads joy and happiness with his dances. He makes people become alive, and appreciate life again. The same way he dances, the Dancing Man passes on the tradition in a circular motion, by the end of the tale in a perpetual manner.

The Folktale

Once upon a time, a young boy called Joseph, lived in Lukulu a market-town somewhere in the world, near a river. Even though Joseph was very young, he was perceptive and could see that there was a lot of unhappiness in the town. Working life seemed to be a daily trudge and chore for its citizens. Life was tough trying to make ends meet. No one ever laughed, joked, smiled or danced in Lukulu.

Joseph himself, young as he was, remained a positive soul and he was able to appreciate all the goodness in the abundance of nature around him. For Joseph, the world around him danced. The flickering flames and sparks from the fire near the town huts jumped and leapt. When Joseph looked at the trees, their arm-like branches swayed to and fro, waving in the wind. Clouds danced in the sky. At night, the stars did a twinkle-toed line-dance.

One-day Joseph was sat by the riverbed and saw an old man there, who had on the most spectacular vibrant silver sandals, and he was dancing amongst the waves. When the old man saw him, he tipped his hat in Joseph's direction, bowed, and said in a sonorous voice,

"I am the Dancing Man. I have a gift for you."

He said, holding out a pair of silver sandals for Joseph to wear.

After Joseph wore them, it was not long before he started dancing, and in doing so he took the old man's place. Joseph went on dancing by the riverbed, then in the village, then amongst all the villages and towns in the whole continent. As he danced, people before who had barely been living, and did not smile or laugh, began to show vitality. An elderly lady who had been practically unresponsive before and had more or less given up on life handed Joseph a beautiful tall sunflower from the side of her chair on the porch. The tall flower with its big yellow head was nearly as tall as Joseph himself. He took the flower as though it were a dancing partner, and wheeled and turned about and spun with it, before lasciviously embrace it. The elderly lady had a fit of giggles.

Joseph met a young girl who was ill and in pain, and as he danced the young girl forgot her illness and smiled, which lit up her face and made her feel better. He met a farmer who was sowing seeds, as he danced, the farmer too joined in and danced as he sowed. The farmer later said that dancing with Joseph made the work more enjoyable and entertaining. Wherever Joseph danced, he brought more life, enthusiasm, passion and amusement to the world.

However, there eventually came a day, when Joseph himself had become old and grew tired. One day, as he was dancing by the riverbed, he looked up and saw a young boy who was standing there watching at him. He had a familiar look on his face, the same look that Joseph himself had all those many years ago. The young boy came closer to him and Joseph knew the words that he had to say. He swept his hat off his head, tipped it at the young boy, before bowing and saying,

"I am the Dancing Man, and I have a gift for you."

20

The Guinea Fowl Child (Pitipiti)

Introduction

The *Guinea Fowl Child* is an African Folktale from Zimbabwe.

This folktale is about marriage, cruelty and vengeance. The story has been relayed orally over the years and is quite popular in East Africa, however, I could not find who captured it on writing for the first time.

It is a Fable about Pitipiti, a woman who was unable to have children and so adopted a Guinea Fowl. The new wife kept on insulting Pitipiti, and in the end, the Guinea Fowl got her revenge.

The Folktale

When Pitipiti was a young girl, she was considered the most beautiful girl in her village. Everyone loved Pitipiti because even though she was pretty, she was also very kind. She fetched water for elderly women and helped widows with housework and farm work. Her parents were poor, but they considered Pitipiti their most important possession because she was also their only child.

Pitipiti's beauty blossomed when she became a young woman, and news of her beauty spread to villages far and near. Young men travelled across rivers and crossed deserts just to see her. Her normally quiet village was now full of suitors who came to beg Pitipiti's hand in marriage. Her old parents had no space in their small hut to house all the gifts Pitipiti's suitors brought.

Pitipiti was nice to all the young men, but she gently turned them down. She wanted to wait for a man who would make her heart dance. Her mother became worried when Pitipiti turned down the three-hundredth suitor – most of them kings of other kingdoms. Mother called Pitipiti and talked to her,

> "You have to choose a husband, my daughter," Mother said.
>
> "It is not wise to turn every one of them away."
>
> "Mother, I will marry when the right man comes," Pitipiti replied, smiling.

"No need to worry, Mother, I have a feeling that I will meet him soon."

One day, a young man came to see Pitipiti's parents about her hand. When Pitipiti was called in to greet the visitor, her eyes met his. She smiled to herself. She knew she had found the love of her life. His name was Dek, and he was a rich farmer. Pitipiti said yes to his proposal, happy that her new husband lived in the neighbouring village and that she would still be close to her parents.

Their wedding was as big as a carnival. The whole village was happy that Pitipiti had found a good man. They knew they would miss her, but as far as she was happy they were happy for her too. The wedding festivities lasted for seven days. They had enough food and drinks to feed three villages. At the end of the seven days of festivities, Pitipiti followed her husband to his village.

Dek loved Pitipiti. Everyone who saw them together could see that their love was very strong. They went everywhere together. During the farming season, they worked on his farm together. Soon, with Pitipiti's help, the couple became even wealthier than before. In a few short years, they became the richest people in the village.

Pitipiti was still a kind woman, and everyday people visited her. No one ever left her house with an empty stomach. Poor people knew they could eat and find shelter in her house. Dek's neighbours in the village came to love her just like she was one of their own. But there was a problem, it seemed that Pitipiti could not have a baby no matter how much she longed for a child.

> "We will have children when the time is right," Pitipiti's husband said to her.

> "Why have not we had a baby by now? We have been

married for years," Pitipiti said, worried that she was never going to achieve her dream of becoming a mother.

Many years passed, taking with them Pitipiti's happiness. People who saw her gloomy face could not believe that she was once a joyful person. She visited many medicine-men in the hopes of ending her problems, but it seemed no one could help her. Dek still loved Pitipiti, but he had grown unhappy about their childlessness. His love for her grew cold. Soon, he began to complain about not having children. And because Pitipiti could not give him the children he wanted, he decided to marry a second wife.

Pitipiti's heart was broken but she could not complain. She danced and celebrated when Dek married a second woman. She still loved Dek, so she rejoiced with him. One year after the wedding, the new wife gave birth to twin babies. One year later, Dek and the new wife welcomed a set of triplets. Pitipiti was happy for them, even though she felt hurt that she would never have her own children. She took gifts to the babies, but the new wife threw the gifts away right in front of Pitipiti.

"We do not want your stupid gifts," the new wife said.

"My husband wasted so many years with you."

Dek did not scold his new wife for insulting Pitipiti. By this time, he no longer loved his first wife. He loved his second wife and his five children, and there was no place for Pitipiti in his heart. Dek took Pitipiti out of their big house, so she moved into a small hut behind. Pitipiti started to age very fast because she was very sad. Her once black hair became as white as salt. Her face sagged because she spent so much time crying. Pitipiti continued to work on the farm. She continued to feed the poor and help the weak. But at night, she cried herself to sleep because she was very lonely. By now Dek and the new wife had ten children. Their big house was always full of laughter. And the new wife continued to mock Pitipiti,

> "You witch," the new wife would say to Pitipiti anytime she saw her.
>
> "Why do not you just die already? Nobody loves you."

Pitipiti never returned her unkind words. She would smile whenever the new wife insulted her, but she would go home and cry in her cold, lonely hut. Dek bought a very large farmland for his new wife, some say it was ten times the size of Pitipiti's farm.

One day, Pitipiti was working on her farm when she heard a strange sound coming from one of the orange trees. She went to check for the sound and found a Guinea Fowl perched on one of the branches of the tree. The Guinea Fowl cried when he saw her,

> "Kind woman, I am very lonely," the Guinea Fowl said, crying.
>
> "Will you take me home with you and make me your son?"

She said no and explained to him that people would mock her for treating a Guinea Fowl as a child. The bird did not stop trying. What Pitipiti did not know was that the Guinea Fowl knew everything about her. The bird had lived on her farm from the time she had married Dek. The bird had watched her transform from a happy woman to one who looked older than her age. The Guinea Fowl liked Pitipiti so much that he would not allow any insect or bird to eat her crops. He sat on a tree in her farm to watch over her. And he always followed her home, he liked to stay on the tree outside her window. That is how he found out that she cried herself to sleep every night.

It hurt the Guinea Fowl that a good woman like Pitipiti lived such a sad life. He felt sympathy for her whenever Dek and the new wife maltreated her. He knew a way to give Pitipiti her heart desire. Therefore, the Guinea Fowl decided to become Pitipiti's son. Since she was afraid of being mocked, he told her that she could make him her child but only at night, that way no one else would know. Pitipiti thought about the Guinea Fowl's request, and she eventually agreed because she also needed someone to keep her company.

The Guinea Fowl visited her at night and left very early in the morning before anyone saw him. She would cook his meals in the evening and the Guinea Fowl would scratch her window, asking to be let in. He would tell her the stories he had gathered flying all over the world, and Pitipiti would feed him and take care of him. They lived as mother and child and enjoyed each other's company. Soon, Pitipiti forgot all her troubles.

The new wife was not satisfied with her own farm, even though it was ten times larger than Pitipiti's. She went to Pitipiti's farm and threatened her,

> "This farm is wasted on you. I will ask my husband to take it from you so that I can add it to mine,"

The new wife said, laughing and walking towards her own farm.

Pititpiti broke down in tears. She had only two things in life: her farm and her Guinea Fowl. And she could not stand the thought of losing any of those things. Her cries attracted the attention of the Guinea Fowl, who was perched on the orange tree in her farm. He was furious that someone had threatened his mother. He could not sit by and do nothing while someone stole from his mother.

The Guinea Fowl flew to the new wife's farm and began to sing this song:

"Come and eat grain on this farm, my friends

This farm has enough grains for all of us."

The new wife heard him sing, but she dismissed it thinking it was ordinary birdsong. The song attracted guinea fowls from far and near and they all descended and ate until there was no grain left on the new wife's farm. The new wife was so angry that she killed all the birds, including Pitipiti's son. She cooked the birds and ate them with her husband. Dek was happy that his new wife had brought home so many birds, so they ate until they could barely move.

They belched and drank water, but as they were ready to clear the table, they heard the song of a Guinea Fowl. They looked around the room, wondering where the song came from. They were shocked when they discovered that the song came from within their stomachs. Scared, Dek and the new wife grabbed knives from their kitchen and stabbed at their own stomachs, hoping to free the birds. The birds escaped from the holes, and the Dek and the new wife fell to the floor, dead. The birds flew to the farm to look for whatever grain they had overlooked.

In the end, Pitipiti's farm prospered and she became even richer. Her beauty and youth returned because no one mocked her anymore. Her son, the Guinea Fowl, no longer had to sneak into her house at night. They lived openly as mother and son.

21

Two Villages

Introduction

The tale of *Two Villages* is an African Folktale from Botswana, in Southern Africa. The country is mainly flat with almost three-quarters covered by the *Kalahari Desert*. One of the major landmarks of Botswana is the *Chobe National Park*, the country first national park with lions and elephants.

This folktale is about team-work, sharing knowledge, change, development and sacrifice. The story has been relayed over the years, and this version has been collected by Rudy Dirks, in *Gaborone*, Botswana capital and largest city.

In this story, you learn of two men with completely contrasting ideas about sharing their knowledge about handicraft skills. One is reluctant to share what he knows, the other will share with anyone interested in learning. One is set in its ways and its craft becomes stilted. The other's craft improves and gets better over time.

The Folktale

Once upon a time, there were two villages, divided by a river that flowed through them. In one of the villages, lived a man called Rra Sephiri (which means Mr Secret). Rra Sephiri was the only person in his whole village who knew how to handcraft beautiful chairs. Whenever anyone in the village needed a chair, they would ask Rra Sephiri to make one. He would never, however, tell anyone his secret as to how they were made. He was scared to pass on his knowledge to others. He worried that other people would not make the chairs as carefully, or accurately as himself. Over time, every chair that existed in the village had been built by Rra Sephiri. Rra Sephiri worried constantly. Rra Sephiri worried in case another person came to the village who was skilled at chair-making and taught others. Because of this worry, he became quite paranoid, and suspicious, if he ever saw anyone so much as carrying wood, he would worry about whether they were going to make a chair. He became quite rude to anyone carrying wood, and would challenge them, make fun of them, and suggest that if they tried to make a chair it would be worthless.

People in the village tried to avoid Rra Sephiri whenever they could. Many people were a bit scared of him because he was so challenging over the slightest thing. People still bought chairs from him, because there was nowhere else to buy them. But, they really tried to limit the time that they spent interacting with him.

Many youngsters would have loved the opportunity to work with him, and to learn his skill of craftsmanship. But, he would never have any of them work for him. He did not want to share his secrets. Many of the youngsters, who he could have trained, left the village to learn crafts and trades elsewhere.

In the other village, that was situated across the river, there was a man called Rra Mosupatsela (also known as Mr Guide). He was a very fine chair-maker too. Rra Mosupatsela however, was not guarded with his knowledge and did not keep it a secret. He wanted other people to learn the skill of chair-making, and to pass on his wisdom and experience to others. He would help anyone who came to him who was interested learn how to make beautiful chairs, the way he made them, and the right places to find good wood. On occasion, a young man who he had taught would find a new way to make an improvement to an existing chair. It could be that he made it sturdier and last longer, or made some adjustment to it to make it more comfortable for the elderly, or simply improved it decoratively. When a young man showed Rra Mosupatsela what he had done, Rra Mosupatsela would encourage him to show others. By doing this, the chairs in this village kept getting better and better as new and improved models came out. People from other villages often came to watch Rra Mosupatsela and his young workers, working together under the big Morula tree. As they worked, they would laugh, joke and tell stories between them.

When people praised Rra Mosupatsela for his wonderful

chairs, he would laugh and say,

> "I did not build these chairs alone. These young men have improved my chairs. I am getting old now, but these young men will continue to build new chairs, better chairs. I have passed on my skills and knowledge to them, and in return, they have given their love, friendship, vision, insight and creativity to me. Together we have done far more than if I had worked alone".

22

The Story of the Wonderful Horns

Introduction

The *Story of the Wonderful Horns* is an African Folktale from South African. It is from the *Xhosa* people, a Bantu subgroup. The *Xhosa* language is South Africa's second-most-populous home language, after the *Zulu* language, to which *Xhosa* is closely related.

The tale addresses several subjects such as magic, kindness, theft, love, honesty, and justice.

Like other orally transmitted stories, there are several versions. This version was captured by George McCall Theall, one of the most prolific and influential South African historian.

The *Story of The Wonderful Horns* is about a boy who received magical horns from his bull. They enabled him to live a rag to riches existence.

The Folktale

There once was a young orphan boy, who had several step-mothers that would not treat him well. His father had died and had left him an Ox. On his deathbed, his father had told him that the Ox was magical and that he should always keep him when travelling, but the young boy did not pay attention.

One day he decided to get far away from his step-mothers who did not treat him well and he set out from his father's home, on the Ox that his father gave him. After a few hours of travel, he and the Ox came across a herd of cattle, that was led by a gigantic ferocious-looking bull. The Ox turned to the young boy and spoke to him,

"I will fight and overcome that bull."

The boy dismounted from the Ox and watched in amazement and disbelief as the fight took place. His Ox won and defeated the gigantic bull. Happy and full of pride, the young boy mounted back his talking Ox, and they rode onwards.

Later that day, the young boy became very hungry. As his stomach was growling, the Ox turned to him and said,

> "Whenever you are hungry, tap my right horn it will provide food for you, tap my left horn and it will take back all that is left."

He tapped the right horn of his Ox, and food came out of it. He ate and satisfied his hunger. He then tapped the left horn to clean the food remaining.

Later that day, they came across another herd of cattle. The Ox then turned to the young boy and said to him,

> "I will fight and die here. You must break off my horns and take them with you. Whenever you are hungry, tap them and they will provide food for you."

In the fight, the Ox was killed as he had predicted. The boy was sad his friend was gone but took the horns as the Ox had said. He continued to travel until he reached a village.

The people in the village were cooking a weed known as Tyutu. That was all that the villagers could eat because there was nothing else. He was invited into one of the houses and got offered to share the Tyutu. The young boy, touched by the hospitality, tapped his horn and enough food came out to satisfy the hunger of the owner of the house and himself. After everybody had eaten, they went to sleep.

During the night, the owner of the house awoke and took the two horns while the young boy was sleeping. He hid them and replaced them with two that looked exactly similar.

The next morning, the young boy woke up fresh and ready to leave. He thanked the owner for his hospitality, of food and a bed for the night and set off on his travels with his horns.

At noon the same day, the young boy felt hungry. He tapped the horns but nothing happened. He tried again and again and again but nothing came out of the horns. The young boy grew suspicious of the owner in the village and decided to return back to the place he had stopped the night before. As he approached the house, he saw the owner frantically tapping and banging and shaking the Ox's horns. Yet, nothing was coming out of them. Tired, the vile owner threw the horns on the ground and left his house to go to the village.

The young boy swiftly recovered his horns and took to his heels to carry on his journey.

He walked for a while, came to another village and stopped at another house. There, he asked the owner if he could eat and stay. To what the owner, after taking a look at the boy, refused and said,

> "Your clothes are ragged, your body is smelly and dirty. Get yourself clean before asking for hospitality."

The young boy looked at himself and recognised that he was dirty and smelly from all his time on the road. He left and went to a river nearby and sat by the bank. He tapped his horns, but this time beautiful clothes fell from the horns. He cleaned himself in the river, wore his new clothes and carried on his journey.

A few hours later, he arrived at a house where there was a beautiful girl. The girl's father was happy to welcome to his house a so well dressed young boy, so he stayed there. With his horns, the young boy was able to provide food and clothing for the entire family.

After some years, the young boy married the beautiful girl. He then took his new wife to his home village. He settled near his father's house and tapped his horns. This time a house came out, and he lived in it with his wife happily.

23

How the Desert Came to Be

Introduction

How the Desert Came to Be is an African Folktale from Ghana.

Like other orally transmitted stories, there are several versions however the origin of this tale is unknown.

It is a mytical story with God and two men, a tale about being faithful and rightful while still being smart.

The Folktale

In a land far away there were once two great farmers. These farmers were said to have giant plots of land as far as the eye could see, their crops stretched as far as the horizon and people would come from far and wide to buy their products. God looked favourably upon these two farmers and soon enough they became very wealthy men. Their names were Kweku Ananse and Akwasi.

Over time these two great farmers got to know each other and soon formed a sort of friendship, as their farms were right next to each other. Now Akwasi was a very good man, he was loyal and trustworthy. But his friend Ananse was not so, Ananse was cunning and sneaky, an incredibly deceiving person that could only be trusted with increasing his own wealth. But they lived in harmony next to each other. Until the day the rain stopped raining, and the crops stopped growing, and the number of buyers started to gradually dwindle.

Eventually, both farmers began to worry as their wealth started to slowly diminish. And so Akwasi decided to go to Nana Nyankopon *"He who knows and sees everything"*, the God of his ancestors to beg for respite from what had to be a punishment for something he did. He cried out saying,

> "Oh, great one what have I done to deserve such punishment? I have always been your faithful servant."

At this, Nana felt pity for the poor mortal and replied,

> "I have grown weary of all your people's small requests and so I decided to entrust different duties to different entities. In your case, I suggest you go visit Nsiah the

hunchback as I have given him the task of rainmaking."

And so Akwasi thanked God and went searching for Nsiah the hunchback.

After some searching, Akwasi found Nsiah the hunchback lying under a giant tree. Nsiah seemed exhausted by his daily task and was resting. Akwasi, being the well-mannered man he was, was reluctant to rouse the poor tired hunchback but was at the thought of his farm immediately walked up to Nsiah and informed him that God had told him to ask Nsiah to send some rain his way. Nsiah reluctantly replied,

"If God has ordered it, who am I to refuse."

And said to Akwasi,

"Tap my back with a small stick and rain will fall upon your land."

Akwasi was quick to do as he was told and after lightly tapping his back, thanked the hunchback, and returned to his home. And sure enough, when he got there he saw that there had been an immense amount of rain, and his farm was looking as green and vibrant as ever.

The next day when Ananse passed by Akwasi's farm and saw that it had rained upon it he cried out in joy, thinking that surely if it had rained on Akwasi's farm it would, without a doubt have rained on his as well. He quickly ran towards his home, excited to see again his beautiful, thriving farm. But to his immense distress, not a single drop of rain had landed on his soil. At this, Ananse was infuriated and cursed God as well as his neighbour, Akwasi. After a long period of anger, he decided to go ask Akwasi what magic he had performed to make it rain on his land. When Ananse asked Akwasi what he had done, Akwasi was reluctant to tell Ananse about his experience with Nsiah the rainmaker, because he knew of Anansi's devious nature. After much inquiry, Akwasi told Anansie how he had managed to get it to rain.

Ananse, determined to regain his wealth and popularity, set out in search of Nsiah the hunchback. Ananse searched for many days and was very worn out by the time he found Nsiah. Nsiah was slumbering beneath the same giant tree that Akwasi had found him under before. But Ananse, being a brute and nothing like Akwasi, grabbed the biggest stick he could find in his immediate vicinity and crept as silently as he could behind Nsiah. Nsiah was so worn out by his taxing job and did not even realize Ananse was behind him until he heard the loud crack of a giant stick striking his bulging back. Even after the hunchback cried out in pain Ananse showed no remorse and continued to beat the unfortunate hunchback as hard as his muscles could manage with such a heavy stick. Soon enough Nsiah's cries turned to whimpers and eventually he was completely silent.

At this point, Ananse, confused, tried yelling at Nsiah,

"GET UP!"

He roared. But there came no response. It took him a while to grasp the fact that he had killed him. He had killed God's rainmaker. Suddenly he was terrified; he could not imagine the punishment that would await him if God found out what he had done. And so he began to consider different ways of escaping the incoming penalty, and he came up with a clever plot to frame his friend Akwasi for the death of the hunchback.

And so Ananse carried the heavy hunchback for a long distance and placed his dead body among the branches of the big tree, he then climbed down and looked up to see if the body was discernible from all the way down there. And to his pleasure, he could not even see the body of Nsiah because of the thick branches of the large mango tree. He then ran quickly to his neighbours' house and told Akwasi to go along with him to the mango plantations so that they would be able to pick out some ripe mangoes before they started to decay. But Akwasi was wary of Ananse and was reluctant to go with him. After a lot of convincing, Akwasi decided to go with Ananse to the mango trees and pick out the fruit.

When they got there, sure enough, the season for mangoes had arrived and they started picking mangoes from the surrounding trees. Ananse was careful not to pick the fruit from the tree in which he had hidden Nsiah because he was waiting for unsuspecting Akwasi to pick from it himself. Soon it was the only tree left that had not been harvested and Ananse said to Akwasi,

> "Go up on the tree and shake it as hard as you can so the mangoes will fall from the tree and they will be easier to pick."

Akwasi thought this was an excellent idea and quickly clambered up the tree and shook it with all his might. After he gave it a few more shakes, he heard an especially loud thump as a body fell from one of the top branches and hit the ground. Akwasi was startled and jumped down from the tree as quickly as he could. By the time he reached the ground, Ananse was fussing about the big hunched body lying face-first on the ground. He looked up and cried,

> "You killed him! You killed the rainmaker."

Akwasi was so shocked that for a few moments he did not know what to think. But slowly, his mind started to piece things together and he understood that he had been tricked by his own friend. Akwasi was not as cunning as Ananse, but he was not a stupid man. And so he started to make a plan of his own, a plan to redeem himself.

Ananse was still yelling at Akwasi, telling him how much trouble he was in. Akwasi acted startled and afraid of the wrath that would await him. He asked,

"How do you think he got up there anyway?"

Ananse, practically squirming with discomfort, became immediately defensive and yelled,

> "How am I supposed to know how a hunchback climbed a tree, it is not like I put him there."

At this, it was very obvious to Akwasi that his friend was the one that killed Nsiah and any doubt he had before disappeared. He calculatingly said to Ananse,

> "I have no choice but to confess my great sin to God and to beg for his forgiveness. Otherwise, if Nana finds out about this himself that I killed his delegate, I will be in even more trouble."

Ananse, upon hearing this, was overjoyed thinking to himself,

> "I have got this fool now, he fell right into my trap."

But out loud he replied,

> "That is a very good idea Akwasi, maybe God will forgive you for your honesty."

Akwasi acted convinced and told Ananse to wait near the mango trees so to protect the body while he went to talk to God. At this Ananse was displeased, but realized it would look suspicious if he was to run away from this task. So he told Akwasi that he would wait for him right there until he returned.

Akwasi ran as fast as he could towards the nearest village, it was a long journey but finally, he made it. Exhausted, he reached the house of the village elder and knocked on his door. The friendly elder, knowing Akwasi very well, gladly welcomed him into his home for some refreshment after a long and tedious journey but Akwasi told the elder that he was in a lot of trouble and was short of time. The elder was shocked because he knew that Akwasi would never get himself into trouble. He asked,

> "My dear friend, I know you are a good man. I can think of no reason you would be in trouble."

Akwasi was emboldened by the amount of trust the elder had in him and told him the whole story, how Ananse had killed the rainmaker and was trying to cheat his way out of the punishment. In the end, Akwasi was left very sad because he had been betrayed by his friend. The elder, however, was furious he exclaimed,

> "How could he do this!"

But Akwasi calmed him down with some tea and soon they were discussing his plan for retaliation.

The first part of the plan was to gather a decent amount of people to be witnesses for any crime that had been committed or may be committed. And so Akwasi and the elder went from house to house, knocking on little mud huts and asking people to come with them to be witnesses. Most of the people were reluctant to come because of the distance they would be walking. But out of respect for the village elder, they came along. Soon they had around ten villagers along with them. And they began their journey toward the mango grove.

They got there a little past midday and sure enough, Ananse was still waiting there, sitting next to the corpse of pitiable Nsiah. Seeing all these villagers, Ananse became very agitated. But kept reminding himself that Akwasi was not a clever man and there was nothing he could possibly think of, as well as the fact that if he ran at that moment they were sure to be very suspicious. And so he sat there and waited for Akwasi to explain to him why he brought so many villagers and even an elder. When the villagers saw the body of Nsiah, they immediately knew who he was and were eager to leave. God should not think they were accomplices to the crime. But the elder assured them it would all be okay, they just had to play along. Akwasi, upon reaching Ananse said proudly,

> "I am very glad you convinced me to go to God Anansi, you have made me a very rich man."

When Anansi heard this he was completely bewildered,

> "Why would the death of the rainmaker make Anansi a rich man," he thought to himself.

But Akwasi answered the unasked question himself,

> "God assured me that Nsiah was a very lazy man and that he was not doing his job well, he was going to take him from his position anyway and because I saved him the hassle, he is rewarding me greatly. These men from the village are here to help me carry the body to God."

Ananse was more than angered by this unexpected turn of events, he was furious, yelling at Akwasi,

> "You idiot! We both know that you did not kill the

hunchback, I killed him myself, when I beat his back so he would give me rain as he gave you."

At this, the elder and the villagers gaped at Ananse, they knew he was a cruel man but had not believed that he could perform such a horrible act. But sure enough, they had all heard his confession. Ananse still did not understand that he had been outsmarted by the man he had underestimated. He ran towards the now rotting body of Nsiah and heaved the heavy hunchback onto his shoulders and said to all of them,

> "I am going to take this dead body to God myself so that I may reap the rewards of my great work, I do not want any of you coming with me so God will think that you helped me in killing this man and reward you also. The reward is mine and mine alone."

Ananse travelled all the way to God's palace, carrying the heavy body on his shoulders. It was a very tiresome journey, but he kept himself motivated by dreams of gold and riches he could not possibly count. Dreams, that little did he know, would never come true. He climbed slowly to the palace of Nana Nyankopon. When he finally reached it, he barged in and called out to Nana. Nana, annoyed by the disturbance, went to check what the frail mortal wanted. When Anansi saw God he was giddy, thinking to himself how pleased God would be with him. But God, upon seeing the dead body of one of his favourite advocate, was furious! But before Nana could say anything Ananse exclaimed,

> "Nana, rejoice for I have killed the lazy hunchback for you. When Akwasi said he was the one who killed him earlier he was lying and was trying to steal my reward from me. The truth is that I murdered him while he was resting under a tree because he was being lazy and not

giving me rain."

Nana, who was at first confused by this, slowly understood what had happened and was enraged by Ananse. As punishment for his transgression, Nana decreed that not a single drop of rain would ever land on Ananse's soil and that it would be cursed so that any crop planted there would wither to nothing and bear no fruit. And that is how the Ghana vast desert came to be.

Afterword

I sincerely hope you enjoyed this book, if so please review it on Amazon: reviews are an author's best friend.

Besides, books worth buying are books worth sharing! I hope you will find someone to give this copy to.

Contact me anytime

The most interesting people I met are the ones I stuck upon randomly. So, if you made it this far, please email me to nwp@email.com say hello. I get really inspired by people's works, so feel free to share your stories, ask me anything, or just tell me what you're writing on. I would be happy to connect.

Made in United States
Orlando, FL
29 April 2025